YAYO 3

S. Allen

2

Lock Down Publications and Ca$h
Presents

YAYO 3

A Novel by *S. Allen*

S. Allen

Lock Down Publications
P.O. Box 944
Stockbridge, Ga 30281

Copyright 2020 by S. Allen
YAYO 3

Lock Down Publications
Like our page on Facebook: Lock Down Publications @
www.facebook.com/lockdownpublications.ldp
Cover design and layout by: **Dynasty Cover Me**
Book interior design by: **Shawn Walker**
Edited by: **Lashonda Johnson**

Stay Connected with Us!

Text **LOCKDOWN** to 22828 to stay up-to-date with new releases, sneak peaks, contests and more…

Thank you!

Submission Guideline.

Submit the first three chapters of your completed manuscript to ldpsubmissions@gmail.com, subject line: Your book's title. The manuscript must be in a .doc file and sent as an attachment. Document should be in Times New Roman, double spaced and in size 12 font. Also, provide your synopsis and full contact information. If sending multiple submissions, they must each be in a separate email.

Have a story but no way to send it electronically? You can still submit to LDP/Ca$h Presents. Send in the first three chapters, written or typed, of your completed manuscript to:

LDP: Submissions Dept
P.O. Box 944
Stockbridge, Ga 30281

DO NOT send original manuscript. Must be a duplicate.

Provide your synopsis and a cover letter containing your full contact information.

Thanks for considering LDP and Ca$h Presents.

Dedication

This book is dedicated to my loving mother, Karen Collins, I will be home real soon. I love you, Mom, you raised a soldier.

Acknowledgments

First and foremost, I want to thank God for giving me this great talent and blessing me with a creative state of mind. It's the key for me to live a wealthy prosocial lifestyle. Shout out to Cash. Fam, you a real nigga and I appreciate you giving me a shot to do what I do with this pen. To all my label mates, too many to name, keep pushing that pen. Special shout out to Jamaica, author of *Last of a Dying Breed*, you did that shorty, your pen game wicked, keep dripping that real. To my potna, Romal Mitchell aka Omega, man fam, you crazy as hell. But you already know shit happens for a reason, we all make mistakes but it's cool as long as we learn from them... I love you, bro. Shout out to Aaron Washington aka Ace from the wild hunnid, Ragtown to be exact, tighten up fam, it's show time and I need you out here with me. We about to make a movie, nigga, straight up! Shout out to Latin King Freddy, much love from one gangsta to another. Shout out to Goon from Jeffrey Manor Projects, P.M.L. Shout out to Larry Hoover for giving me a vision that molded me into the man I am today and teaching the concept of Growth and Development. Without these teachings, I would be lost. Free Larry. For y'all that don't know who Larry Hoover is, he is a great man. Last, but not least, thanks to all my friends and readers that support my work. It is you who I do this for.

S. Allen

S. Allen

CHAPTER 1

"Alright, Mr. B, I'm about to bounce up outta here so I can make this move," YaYo said, logging off the computer. He had been working and typing up his manuscript called *Drill Season*. It had been eighteen months since he was in the Federal Court Building, Downtown Chicago, handing his life sentence back to the federal government. Even though he was found not guilty on some of the charges, one charge stuck. And that was the possession of a firearm in which he was given one hundred and twenty months, ten years to be exact. With YaYo already having served four years, he could only have to give the feds four more years if he stayed outta trouble and out the way. While USP Pollock was on an institution lock-down, YaYo found his hidden talent as a writer. He had always wanted to write an urban novel after reading several books from a publisher called Lockdown Publications. So, he figured he would give it a shot. Mr. B was very supportive of YaYo and his vision and took the job as YaYo's editor. Mr. B was proud that YaYo was doing something constructive with his time. So, Monday through Friday, YaYo and Mr. B would spend at least three hours in the law library. YaYo would be typing away on his manuscript and Mr. B would be doing or finishing up law work.

It was 12:30 in the afternoon when the move was called. YaYo left the library en route to his unit, C-1. It was ninety-three degrees outside, good weather in Pollock, Louisiana, as on an average day the heat index could reach a hundi, or one-hundred-plus degrees. The prison yard was in full swing with crowds of inmates involved in recreation! Activities such as playing basketball, exercising, or playing softball. Some inmates just walked the track, trying to get a peace of mind and away from the grueling day-to-day life of being in a federal penitentiary. Then, there were those who let evil, be-trayal and deceit cloud their mind frames as they indulged them-selves and their time into heavy prison politics. It was always dif-ferent strokes for different folks.

After clearing the metal detectors, YaYo walked into his unit. C-1 was considered the worst unit in Pollock because a lot of the violent incidents came from there. Pollock was a breeding ground for violence. There were so many violent crimes in the prison, the institution was always locked down, which was hectic for C.O.'s, because the correctional officers would now have to perform the job titles reserved for the inmates. Such as feeding the population, sanitation of the prison as well as other things. The administration came up with a strategic idea. Whatever unit the incident happened in, the captain of the prison would have that unit locked down, instead of the whole prison. So, C-1 was almost always locked down. due to some work call. YaYo hated his living conditions but had adapted well to prison life. He had developed a daily routine, which consisted of all righteous endeavors. In the morning when the doors popped at 5:45, he would get dressed and make "Salat". At 8:45, he would go to school. Mr. B had told YaYo over and over, education was power. So, he enrolled in numerous classes on building maintenance, HVAC as well as GED classes. YaYo would then go to lunch and from there, he would go to the law library with Mr. B and work on his book. Any time after 12:30 was free recreation for him, which he chose to use to exercise his mind. YaYo walked over to the computer to check his email. After logging in to his CorrLinks account, he saw that he had three emails. One from his wife Shakira, one from his mother, and one from his lil brother, Davon. He read Davon's email first.

"What's good with you, Big Bro? I was just checking on you. Don't think I forgot to send you those magazines. I got you. I just been a little busy. I may put them in the mail tonight. I got you a *Phat Puff*, a *Don-Diva*, and this new magazine called *Gangstas* and *Bosses*. It got the board member for his GD's on the cover. His name, Crusha. Oh yeah, I saw Quavon a couple days ago. That dude off the chain fam, told me he's just wrecked a Dodge Demon! Holla at you, lil bro."

YaYo shook his head, thinking about how Quavon was out there in the streets. He had heard from niggas coming into the federal system fresh off the streets that his lil bro was out there cutting up. He was getting a lot of money and his crew was putting in plenty work. YaYo felt guilty about how Quavon's life had turned out. He

10

had given Quavon the jewels to excel in the dope game and now he was turned out. Quavon wants it all. YaYo just kept Quavon in his prayers and asked God not to let Davon fall into the same vicious deadly cycle that he and Quavon did.

YaYo was proud of Davon. He had proved a lot of people wrong. Doctors and medical staff had said Davon would never walk again. With good therapy sessions and Davon's drive and willingness, he was able to overcome his trial and tribulations. After graduating college, Davon was able to land a job at EA-Sports as a video game technician and was getting paid handsomely, twenty-five dollars an hour. Davon even had his own apartment on 81st and Drexel. Things were looking up for Davon and YaYo couldn't wait for his release, so he could go home and kick it with his lil brother.

YaYo read Shakira's email next. "Hey baby, how is your day going? I hope it's fine. I got your lil freak letter last night! LOL. Baby, you are so nasty…I can't wait 'til you come home so you can do all those things to my body. Lord knows I need it. But anyways, tell me why I had to go up to Shamira's school today to find out your daughter had a fight with another lil girl. The principal all mad and shit, talking about Shamira has an attitude problem and I should consider putting her in an alternative school. I looked at him like he was crazy…Shit, all five-year-old's have an attitude. So, when Shamira got in the car, I asked her what happened and she said the girl was making fun of her saying, 'Ah-ha your daddy in jail.' So, she said she slapped the girl. Can you please call home tonight to talk to your daughter? Plus, I want to hear your voice. I love you."

YaYo couldn't believe what he had just heard about his little princess getting into her first fight, over somebody disrespecting him at that. It hurt his heart to know his five-year-old daughter was over there going through that, all because of him and the choices he made when he was on the streets. But at the same time, he was proud of her love and loyalty to him. Things would be different once he came home, he would be able to talk, hold and console his loved ones. He would make sure his precious little girl would be protected and well taken care of. As of right now, he could do nothing but pray to the all merciful Allah to look over his family and their well-being, and his strong faith was telling him Allah would not fail him.

YaYo read his mother's email last. "Yaton, how are you doing son? I hope fine and in good spirits as you should. Your grandmother's eighty-third birthday is coming up! I can't believe my mother is eighty-three, but I tell you one thing, she is one of the sharpest knives in the drawer. She always wants things her way and if it's not done the way she wants, she is definitely going to make a big fuss about it, LOL. I forgot to tell you, Darrell has found a nice house in Orlando, Florida. He was thinking about moving down there. He wants to start a business down there, but I wanted to talk to you about it first. Whenever you get the chance, give me a call so we can talk. I love you and miss you, son!"

YaYo thought about what his mom just said. Florida was a long way from Chicago and the fact that she was moving down there with Darrell really didn't sit right with him. Since YaYo had given the life sentence back, Darrell had flown to Louisiana to visit him. He was shocked when his mother had told him Darrell needed a visit form so he could get placed on his visit list. And he was reluctant to send him one, but YaYo wanted to face the past and see what the man who destroyed his life had to say to him.

When he walked into the prison visiting room, he spotted Darrell immediately. HIs hair was now salt and pepper, he had lost a little weight, but his facial features had remained the same. Darrell's Tom Ford suit looked expensive and the Ferragamo loafers that adorned his feet matched perfectly with the suit. He could have been on the cover of *GQ*.

When YaYo walked up to Darrell at the back table, his chest began to tighten up and his aggression level began to rise. He didn't know if he should shake his hand or break his jaw in three different places. Darrell noticed YaYo's clenched fist and chose his words carefully before he spoke.

"Trust and believe I know how you feel," Darrell spoke, humbly putting his hands out palms up. "You have every right to feel how you feel about me, but all I ask is that you give me a few minutes to explain myself."

"You got a lot of nerve, my nigga. But you don't have a lot of time, so if I was you, I would start talking." YaYo sneered.

"Yaton, all I really came here to tell you is that I am truly sorry for how I treated you. When I got with your mother, you were already born into the world. I had to take on the responsibility of fatherhood. Something I knew nothing about. How could I be a father to a child and mentally I was a child myself? When I got your mom pregnant and she had twins, I was the proudest father in the world. I loved them with all my heart. All my love went to them and in my immature mind frame, you didn't matter to me anymore, because you weren't my blood.

"I didn't know how to love you all the same, and all the problems that were coming my way as far as with all the bills and my job, I released my stress on you and I know I was wrong for that. I should've never sent you to Chicago like that. Had I not done that, you wouldn't have ended up in this shit hole."

YaYo saw the tears roll down Darrell's cheeks. He could see the pain and guilt etched all over his stepfather's face. The words he had just spoken sounded genuine and from the heart. Even though YaYo had humbled himself since he walked in the visiting room, he felt he still had to keep his gangsta up. The fact of the matter still remained that Darrell had played a major part in how YaYo's life turned out.

Had YaYo not been sent to live in the poverty-stricken streets of Chi-Raq, he would've never been exposed to the criminal element that molded him into a murdering drug dealer and gang chief. The streets of the Chi had taken an innocent child and turned him into a thoroughbred goon and his outcome, if not his identity, had landed YaYo in the depths of a United States penitentiary.

"You know, I used to respect you and I looked up to you like a father. But after all the bullshit you put me through in my life, nigga, I wanted to kill your ass. The first life I took, I imagined it was your face I put that bullet in. That's some crazy shit, huh?" Darrell lowered his eyes in front of the killa that sat before him. YaYo's dialog alone sent chills down through his spine. YaYo continued. "The only reason you still breathing is because you my lil brother's father and if something was to happen to you it would crush them. Those two niggas are my heart and when they feel pain, I feel pain. And even though you abused my mother physically and mentally, for some reason, she loves you. And unlike you, I would never want to see her hurt."

"Yaton, all I can do is say I am sorry, and I am a changed man. If I could turn back the hands of time, Yaton, I would. God knows I would, and when it's all said and done, the good Lord will make sure I'm punished for all of my sinful ways."

"Looks like to me he was blessing you," YaYo said sarcastically, looking over the expensive suit Darrell was rocking.

"Well, he has definitely blessed me financially. My business is starting to expand, so things are looking up."

YaYo sat with his arms crossed in front of him. "So, let's get straight to the point. Why are you down here, Darrell? I know it ain't just to apologize and shed them big ass chocolate tears."

"Yaton, I just want your forgiveness, a chance to make things right between us. I love you, man, and we family."

"Family, huh?" If you were family, my nigga, you wouldn't have played shit how you played it. But I ain't trippin. I love the man I turned out to be, I'm stronger than you'll ever be. You'll never be the man I am, in prison or the free world. You a weak nigga to me, an abusive, jealous, simple-minded motherfucker. I have been learning that Allah forgives, so if the all merciful Allah forgives, then I can forgive. But I will never forget. I appreciate you coming down here and all, but they are about to serve chow. They're serving my favorite, some watered-down spaghetti."

YaYo got up, leaving Darrell sitting down and drowning in his guilt. When YaYo got back to the unit, he got on the computer and noticed he had ten stacks, just put on his account, from Darrell. The money meant nothing to YaYo. Seeing Darrell face-to-face and getting everything off his chest took some of the weight off his shoulders, and the ten thousand on his book didn't hurt either. Long as Darrell was out there making sure his mama and lil bro's was good, he was straight for now.

YaYo took about fifteen minutes to email his family back. He was glad everybody was alright. Things were going good for YaYo, he had good family support, he only had about three years to the door and he was stacking up his money in the joint so when he was released, he wouldn't have to ask anybody for anything, he would be his own safety net. After emailing his loved ones, YaYo raced up to his cell to change into his sweatpants, to get ready for the 1:00 move so he could get his workout in. So far it had been a nice, peaceful day. But in USP Pollock, a sunny cloudless day could easily turn into a shadowy, gloomy, violent night.

CHAPTER 2

YaYo had just come in from outside rec. Making his way up the tier, he saw B.D. Pook involved in a spades game. He noticed B.D. Pook being animated as hell, but that was Pook. Always loud, talking shit and being B.D. Pook, so YaYo paid it no mind. Grabbing his shower things, YaYo made his way to the shower.

Once in the small confined shower box, YaYo undressed, stuck his shank in the crack in his wall and turned the shower on, the hot water seemed to relax his tight muscles. He had just completed a vicious workout called the Furious-Five, which consisted of three hundred Navy Seal push-ups, three hundred burpees, three hundred push-ups, three hundred jumping jacks, three hundred crawl outs, and three hundred kickouts.

YaYo had learned this workout from a GD named Bible, who was from Chicago, the Englewood Area, close to YaYo's hood on 69th and Walcott. In the federal penitentiary, staying in shape was a must, due to the violence. The key to survival in the USP was to be militant minded and remain to be T.T.G, aka Trained to Go. YaYo soaped up his body as he let his mind drift momentarily outside of the prison walls, as he thought about what he was going to say to his daughter when he called her tonight. He didn't want her to grow into a criminal life, but at the same time, he wanted her to be strong and never bullied or pushed over.

After YaYo dried off, dressed and put his shank in the slit in the front of his boxers and made his way to his cell. On the way, he looked at the activity that was taking place in the dayroom. He could see the Alabama inmates, thirteen in all, standing in front of a cat's cell named Boogaloo, who was from Mobile, Alabama. YaYo figured they had something going on within their own crew. After putting on a fresh sweat suit and a pair of black Air Force One's, YaYo tied his long dreads into a ponytail with a thick rubber band. He exited the cell on his way to the phone to call his daughter.

Listening to the phone ring, YaYo watched as B.D. Pook came out of his cell, the look on his face menacing. His eyes were blood-shot, and both of his hands were in his pockets. Another homie named Harold trailed behind him, his facial expression identical to B.D. Pook's.

Looking around the dayroom, YaYo now knew it was some major tension and from looks of it all, B.D. Pook and Harold definitely had something to do with it. YaYo hung up the phone just as Shakira had accepted the call. B.D. Pook reached the bottom of the steps where YaYo stood. YaYo grabbed his hands. "What's good, fam? You good, my nigga?" YaYo asked, fully concerned about his man's.

"Watch out!" B.D. Pook said through clenched teeth, yanking his arm out of YaYo's grasp, making his way over to the crowd of Alabama inmates. YaYo saw Harold going in the trash can, where they hid their knives. YaYo's heart began to beat fast as he followed B.D. Pook to the drama about to unfold.

"Man, y'all chill. We all cool up here. Y'all leave that shit alone," Muggsy, an Alabama cat said, trying to keep the peace. The Alabama inmates stood behind him with mean mugs on their hardened faces. A few of them held locks tied to belts.

Boogaloo stepped from the circle and walked up to B.D. Pook and sneered. "What you come down here with your hands in your pocket for, like you gone pop something."

"You said you wanna see? See me then, pussy!" B.D. Pook said through clenched teeth before he pulled the small shank from the confines of his pants pocket and stabbed Boogaloo in the chest. Boogaloo felt the cold piercing feeling from the steel entering his flesh and realized he had just been stabbed, and grabbed his chest and quickly backpedaled to get away from the gangsterous situation he was now involved in.

Harold pulled a ten-inch bone crusher from the garbage can and yelled, "Work call!" And started to rush the Alabama niggas who was now trying get somewhere after seeing their big homie get hit up. The sight of blood made them turn the volume down on their fuckery.

"Man, I ain't got nothing to do with that, my nigga," An Alabama dude by the name of Thug said to YaYo, before YaYo punched him in the jaw. Thug's adrenaline was rushing, and not trying to go out like a sucka, he swung back at YaYo. Ducking the frivolous attempt, YaYo pulled his knife from his boxers, connecting the end of the knife to Thug's face. Thug took off running with his face leaking from the wound that had just been inflicted.

The dayroom was in pandemonium, all you could hear was chairs getting knocked over and gym shoes screeching on the ground. YaYo, B.D. Pook and Harold chased the Alabama inmates around the dayroom, stabbing and punching anything and anyone who was from Alabama, until the officer in the officer's station saw the assault and hit the body alarm.

"Charlie 1... I repeat, Charlie 1 inmates fighting with weapons. I repeat, inmates fighting with weapons!" A minute later, Unit C-1 was swarmed with correctional officers with riot pumps and tear gas. They were a tad bit late. YaYo had made his way to his cell as B.D. Pook and Harold ditched their bloody knives in the trash and ducked off into the safety of their cells.

"Step in a cell now! Step in a fucking cell!" the C.O. yelled, telling all inmates to lock in a cell. Boogaloo stood in front of his cell, his face and sweatshirt bloody as he held his shank in his hand. He had been punished. Not adhering to the C.O.'s command, they rushed him and wrestled the weapon away from, him and took nine to the Special Housing Unit. After securing the unit, the C.O.'s went cell to cell, conducting body searches in an attempt to get all that was involved in the altercation. YaYo pulled the knife out his pocket and tossed it in the toilet and flushed. The weapon remained at the bottom of the toilet.

"Shit," he cursed. He had to get rid of the weapon, but the correctional officers were now three cells away. He had to think fast. Going into his locker, he grabbed a razor and made a slit in the corner of his pillow and tucked the shank in it, folded a blanket around the pillow and put it neatly in the chair inside the cell and placed the chair by the door, just as the C.O.'s opened his cell door.

"Alright, we are going to ask you to step to the back of the cell." YaYo did as instructed. "Take your shirt off and stick your hands out." YaYo obliged. The officers examined YaYo's upper torso. "Turn around," the C.O. commanded with authority. YaYo turned around, giving the C.O.'s visual of his back. Seeing no wounds or scars from aggression, the C.O. ordered YaYo to turn back around.

"Let me see your hands, boy." YaYo stuck his hands out. "Turn them slowly." YaYo turned his hands over now exposing his palms. "He has blood on his hands He is involved Cuff this inmate," the C.O. said, noticing the specks of dried up blood on the inside of YaYo's right palm, the same palm that held the six-inch piece of sharpened steel he was just working with. YaYo looked at his hand and couldn't believe he had literally got caught red-handed.

YaYo was cuffed and escorted to the SHU. On the way out the unit, he looked around the dayroom that looked like Hurricane Katrina had just swept through. Tossed over chairs and dried blood stains covered the floors. It was another day in USP Pollock. Once in the SHU, YaYo was placed in a small bullpen to be processed.

"Mr. Anderson, what's going on? What was that all about? Was it over disrespect, a debt? What happened?" S.I.S. Lieutenant Crab asked. S.I.S. Crab was in charge of investigations in the prison. S.I.S. stood for Special Investigation Service. YaYo had taken a life sentence because he lived by the G-code and snitching wasn't in his bloodline, so he remained silent.

"So, I see you still holding on to the code of the streets, huh? I'm fine with that, asshole, but guess what, Mr. Integrity? The guy we got you on video footage stabbing, he had to take a Med-Life flight up outta here. The ambulance would have gotten here too late You know it still might be a little too late." YaYo remained stone-faced.

"I'm making sure you rot back here in this motherfucka," Lieutenant Crab said, leaving YaYo standing there. YaYo was processed and put on Range 3 of the SHU. special housing unit. He was placed in the cell with a Blood gang member whose name was G-Wayne. G-Wayne was from Detroit, Michigan, and was serving a twenty-year sentence for six jewelry store robberies. YaYo knew G-Wayne from the compound and was always cool with the young cat.

"What's up, Blood?' G-Wayne greeted YaYo once he was locked in the cell.

"Ain't shit, niggas jumped out there," YaYo retorted, throwing his mattress on the top bunk.

"That was y'all out there working? We heard the deuces go off. Who y'all get into it with?" G-Wayne probed.

"Weak ass Alabama niggas, with all that fakin and shit."

"Me, Pook, and Latin Folks Harold."

"Damn, straight up?"

"Hell, yeah. I still don't know why Pook took off. So, you already know how that go."

"Yeah, I'm already hip, my nigga. You good tho, Blood? I got food and hygiene in here, we ain't going to commissary 'til next Tuesday."

"Yeah, that's what up." YaYo and G-Wayne were chopping it up. YaYo had found out G-Wayne was back in the SHU for getting caught with a knife, and was scheduled to be released back to the compound in two weeks. While the two gangsters were caught up in conversation, S.I.S. Crab came to the cell door.

"Hey, Anderson, come to the door."

What the fuck this mag want? YaYo thought, walking out the door.

"Guess what, asshole? Rodney Simpson, the guy we have you on video repeatedly stabbing? .Well he didn't make it. He expired, dummy. So, I guess the government will be able to hand you back that life sentence. I'll keep you posted, dipshit," was all Lieutenant Crab said before he left YaYo. His breath was taken away and his life was flashing before his eyes. He had just caught a jail house murder. He would never get a chance to raise her daughter. He'd never be able to hold his child's mother. His mother was going to be crushed, knowing her oldest son would never walk the streets again, a free man. YaYo felt like he was about to throw up. When he was sliding the knife, he wasn't attempting to kill, but his adrenaline took him to another level as his inner demon was unleashed, causing a fatality.

"What that faggot just say, Blood?" G-Wayne said, bringing YaYo out of his trance.

"That nigga just said I killed shorty," YaYo replied. His life was over.

"Damn, B., That's fucked up, my nigga." G-Wayne fucked with YaYo hard and knew YaYo was getting released back to society in a few years. To him, YaYo was a good dude who was always preaching positivity, growth and development. YaYo would always tell him that economical, political, and social development was key to a pro-social lifestyle. YaYo was always talking about positive change. He knew YaYo wasn't a soft nigga as his street reputation and paperwork matched perfectly with the character of a certified street nigga. G-Wayne looked up to YaYo and now felt his pain.

YaYo got on the top bunk and put his pillow over his face to hide his tears from the world. His mind was blank, he had no words at this point, his soul was gone. Like a baby, YaYo cried himself to sleep.

CHAPTER 3

Quavon slid through mid-day traffic in his Audi A7. Rockett occupied the passenger seat. They were on their way to meet up with a financial investor, who Quavon named Bank Roll Buddy.

Quavon was a regular in Tampa. He had met a chick named Bella who was sweating his Instagram. Bella was a Dominican chick who came from long money. Her father was a stock market giant that spoiled her rotten.

Quavon was a street nigga with plenty of prestige, but it was Bella who put him on the next level of the game. Quavon had much swag, as his closet was flooded with Balmain, Givenchy and Rockstar jeans, and Jordan's, but Bella introduced him to Tom Ford, Ferragamo, and Michael Kors. Quavon had even stepped his jewelry up, now instead of Jacob & Co. watches, Ulysee Nardin and Louis Moinet pieces surrounded his wrist.

Bella was a piece that fitted the puzzle. She was beautiful and at five-eleven, her Coke-bottle shape plus her exotic facial features gave her the Kim Kardashian look. She could have any man she wanted. She followed Quavon on his Instagram and loved his thugged-out, doe-boy swag. She knew Quavon was a hustler, because in all his pictures on Instagram, he was posted with stacks and stacks of dead presidents. Once she got with Quavon, she was hooked, his swag and dick game were up to par. She knew Quavon was on his way to the top, so she figured she would give him an extra push up the success ladder.

Bella and Quavon met Bank Roll Buddy, whose name was Robert Johnson, at an upscale restaurant in Tampa. Robert had introduced himself as a financial advisor and gave Quavon his info. Quavon also found out Robert had many underworld connections and he was able to move large sums around. Subsequently, Quavon used Robert for monetary reasons, and whenever Bella let him smell her womanly scent, he appeared with unlimited monetary wishes. Quavon looked down at his Louis Moniet timepiece and realized he was running late.

"So, what's good with Bank Roll Buddy?" Rockett asked from the passenger seat.

"I'm about to holla at his nigga about doing this movie shit. Lionsgate playing games with the stash house flick. They said they liked the manuscript and they wanted eight hundred large to produce the film, now they saying they need one point five and they want they own actors. Ain't no way, my nigga, they taking away from my creativity, feel me?"

"Yeah, I feel you, shawty, so what are you gonna do now?"

"That's what I'm about to holla at Bank Roll Buddy about. I already gave these pussy ass niggas the eight and the manuscript. I don't want to pull all the way out and then they try and use the stash house idea, feel me?"

"Yeah, I dig it, shawty."

"They already fake played us on the Lil Durk movie. Shit, after we paid dude, we barely broke even. So, I'm a see if Bank Roll Buddy can finesse these dudes."

"Oh, before I forget, my nigga, I already hollered at Crusha and Reggie-G about this, but they told me to holler at you."

"Speak on it, family," Quavon replied as he pulled the A7 into the parking lot of Fox's Jewelers and parked beside a cocaine-white S Class Benz.

"You know shawty and them in Memphis?"

"Yeah. What's up?"

"Well, they ain't been shopping like they supposed to be. Word on the streets is they been getting they work from the some nigga name Suge. They say his prices are cheaper, but the work ain't hittin on nothing."

"Them the niggas from Berry Homes, right?"

"Yeah, them niggas, shawty."

"Well, you tell them they need to get their coke from G.B.C. Tell 'em we keeping the prices the same, but we got more bricks for them. If they buck that, then blow that bite." Rockett nodded his head in understanding. Quavon was his boss and he was subordinate to his leadership. "By the way, find out who that nigga Suge is, get with that nigga and let him know we got it for the low. He got on some cocky shit, bust his shit to the white meat," Quavon ordered.

Quavon and the G.B.C. was getting plenty of money. After robbing Top-Cat and killing him for a three kilos of uncut heroin, it was no turning back for him and his men. After swiftly selling the kilos, Quavon took a gamble with life and returned back across the border to give Castilino, leader of the Madina Cartel, his money. Every red penny of it.

Castilino was a little shocked that Quavon had shot and killed Top-Cat. When he asked Quavon why he had murdered his boss, Quavon smoothly replied that Top-Cat was a stagnation in his growth. Plus, Top-Cat disrespected him and the G.B.C. by having him kidnapped. So, his lie was on borrowed time from that point forward. Castilino had seen the hunger and ambition in his eyes and knew it would be just a matter of time before Quavon would make a move to become his own boss.

Since doing business with Quavon, his money was always brought on time, not to mention Quavon was moving more weight than Top-Cat and his crew. Quavon's recipe for financial growth was complete dominance and control. It was either get down or lay down. Not only was Quavon pushing a hard line in the streets of Chicago, but other major cities as well. With Memphis, Tennessee being one of his most lucrative spots that he flooded with heroin and cocaine, Quavon had claimed Memphis as G.B.C. territory and those that went against the laws of his land was eliminated ASAP.

The G.B.C. had grown into a force to be reckoned with. Most of Top-Cat's soldiers, after his demise, signed up with the G.B.C. Those that chose to remain loyal to Top-Cat and his politics were put on the WGN 9:00 news. Even though many of the thugs in Chicago claimed to be members of G.B.C., Quavon only trusted his inner circle which was the chain of command. Choppa, Rockett, Reggie-G and Crusha was his team. Only their opinion mattered within the G.B.C. infrastructure, with Choppa and Rockett being his designated hitters. If you fucked up Quavon's paper and he sent Rockett or Choppa, it was no discussion, just the sounds of gun clapping.

Quavon and Rockett got out the Audi A7. Rockett adjusted the compact .45 ACP on the waist of his Balmain's.

"Bank Roll Buddy. What's the bizness, my dude?" Quavon greeted, extending his hand to Bank Roll Buddy, who was standing beside the cocaine-white Benz.

"Same ol' shit, Quavon, chasing the money," Bank Roll Buddy replied.

"See, that's your problem, big homie. You chase the money, instead of letting the money chase you. Wasn't you the one that told me money doesn't lead?"

"I see you listen, youngsta."

"Why wouldn't I listen and take your advice? You a fucking millionaire." `

"Yeah, whatever. If I keep messing with you, I'll be on Wacker Drive with a cardboard sign that says will work for food." The men erupted in laughter. "Enough of the small talk, shall we get to the importance of this meeting?" Bank Roll Buddy said and led the way to the jewelry store. Bank Roll Buddy pushed the buzzer in front of Fox's Jewelers. They were buzzed in. Bank Roll Buddy was part-owner of the jewelry store. A beautiful, exotic female sat behind the counter. "Maria, how are you my dear?"

"I'm good, how are you, Mr. Johnson?"

"Listen, I'm going to be in the bank taking care of some business, can you please entertain our friend?" Bank Roll Buddy replied, motioning towards Rockett.

"No problem, sir," Maria replied, letting her eyes roam over Rockett.

"Quavon, this way, my friend." Bank Roll Buddy led Quavon to his office located in the back, leaving Rockett with Maria. Once in the back office, Bank Roll Buddy went over to a small mini bar and poured two hosts of Crown Royal Black and handed one of the glasses to Quavon. "Shall we make a toast, Quavon?"

"To what?"

"To power and wealth, my friend." The two men hit glasses and downed the liquor. Quavon felt the strong cognac go through his bloodstream, feeling its effect immediately.

"So, what seems to be the problem, Quavon?" Bank Roll Buddy asked after downing the rest of his shot.

"The problem is these thirsty motherfuckers at Lionsgate."

"I'm listening." Bank Roll Buddy walked back over to the bar to retrieve the bottle of Crown Royal.

"You already know they fucked us on the thing we did with Lil Durk, a nigga damn near was about to have to come out our pocket to pay shorty. Now they on some bullshit with Stash House."

"What do you mean, bullshit?" Bank Roll Buddy refilled their shot glasses.

"They say instead of the eight hundred bands we gave them, now they say we need to come up with one point five."

"Why is that a problem? We can come up with the money."

"That ain't even all of it. They say they're going to come up with their own actors."

"How is that?"

"That's what the fuck I'm saying, nigga. I'm tired of these dudes tryna lil boy a nigga."

"Why not just pull out and say fuck it?"

"Because they already got the fucking script. I don't want them to fucking steal it. I didn't get the script copywritten."

"Quavon, are you fucking nuts? You can't be that stupid, kid."

"Watch your fucking mouth," Quavon said, through clenched teeth, ready to smash his shot glass against Bank Roll Buddy skull for his minor disrespect.

"All I'm saying, Quavon, is that...that wasn't smart. What do you want me to do?"

"What I want is for you to go over there to Lionsgate Films and get some kind of understanding with them. Let them know we are not giving them no more bread, we are using our own actors and we are moving forward with the film."

"What if they don't go for it?"

"If they don't get with the program, you let me know. I just wanted to send you over there to try and talk some sense into their heads before I handled shit my way," Quavon said, downing his shot. If Lionsgate wanted to act like they were buying the G.B.C., they had another thing coming.

"So, how much are these, lil shawty?" Rockett asked, admiring the one carat L'Amour Crisscut diamond earrings he held in his palms. Maria walked from around the counter. When Rockett saw how thick she was, his meat began to swell. As Maria walked up to Rockett, his Gucci cologne invaded the airwaves. His long dreads were braided into six braids. The ice on his neck hung to the middle of his chest, connected to a large Jesus piece charm sprayed with ice. She was definitely attracted to him. She took the earrings out of his hand.

"These, my dear, are from Christopher Designs. It's only ten of these sets in the world. This set is fifty thousand large. Your girl-friend or wife would love to have these," Maria said seductively.

"I ain't got neither of them, shawty, I'm married to these streets," Rockett replied with a thuggish demeanor that only seemed to turn her on even more. Stepping up in his personal space, Maria grabbed his crotch and gave it a slight squeeze, before she leaned in and kissed him.

Their tongues explored each other's mouths while Rockett groped her gigantic ass cheeks. Maria led Rockett behind the counter, where she got on her knees. After unbuckling his Gucci belt, she pulled his Balmain's down. Reaching in his Tom Ford boxers, Maria freed Rockett's ten-inch, thick, veiny cock. She couldn't believe the width of his monstrous dick. Hungrily, she engulfed as much as she could. It looked like a black dill pickle was in her mouth.

Rockett almost shot his hot load down her throat from the warmth of her mouth and the thickness of her tongue. Rockett grabbed a fist full of her naturally curly black hair, looking down at the beautiful face, he started pumping in and out of her mouth, fuck-ing her face. Maria was jerking on his pole with both hands and her moaning drove Rockett crazy and he couldn't control it as he shot a load off in her mouth in three strong spurts, causing her to gag. Ma-ria tried to swallow as much as she could. What she couldn't, seeped out the corner of her mouth onto her shirt.

"Damn, shorty!" Rockett said, pulling his jeans back up. Maria wiped the leftover semen off her mouth with the back of her hand and stood up. Straightening her short skirt, she took her spot back behind the counter, just as Quavon and Bank Roll Buddy came from the back office.

"So, I will give you a call, Quavon, once I hear back from Lionsgate."

"Yeah, you make sure you do that." Quavon and Rockett left the jewelry store. Once inside the A7, Quavon asked Rockett. "So, what's up with the sexy lil bitch back there, you smash?"

"Naw, shawty," Rockett said as he slid out of the parking lot.

"Nigga, stop lying. The bitch still had cum on her shirt." Both men laughed. Getting plenty of pussy was the norm for the G.B.C. They ran the city and were getting all the money. They were at the top of the dope game, but only time would tell if they would remain in that position of power.

CHAPTER 4

"They say the authorities have no suspects or no leads to the crime."
KI said, looking at the news clipping on her phone. They had gotten
away with a robbery and a murder in Tennessee when they robbed
a gun store, leaving a man shot to death inside the store. The Homicide Crew was at a trap spot on the south side, politicking about
their future murderous endeavors. Omega, Ace, Goon, and Marcus
were all in attendance. KI tossed her iPhone on the couch and fired
up this blunt of sour diesel Kush she had just rolled. After taking a
strong pull from the blunt, she passed it to Omega, held the smoke
in her lungs for a minute before she blew the smoke out her nostrils.

"Now, let's go over this shit one more time. I'm a meet the nigga
at the Cheesecake Factory at the Ford City Mall. Once we finish
eating, I tell him to get a room at the Congress. Goon, you and Marcus follow us to the hotel and once we pull up in the parking lot,
y'all make the move and snatch the nigga up and bring him back
here. Omega, you and Ace be waiting here at the spot. Once the
nigga give us the info, I'm a go get it. After that, y'all niggas already
know what to do." KI said, going over the plans for the lick they
had set up.

The target was a mid-level heroin dealer named Roy. KI had
met Roy at a nightclub in downtown Chicago. She had spotted him
from across the room because the jewelry decorating his neck, wrist
and ears were demanding attention from the shine. Roy had on at
least two hundred thousand dollars' worth of ice. His body was
draped in Marc Jella and his aura alone represented wealth. KI made
her way over to the bar, where Roy and some of his men were
chilling and enjoying the scene.

"Excuse me, can I get a bottle of Apple Cîroc?" KI said to the
bartender as she stood on her tippy toes in her red bottoms. Her Vera
Wang jeans hugged her curvaceous body so tight, it looked as if the
jeans were painted on her. Her hair was in a short bob, giving her
Robert Coin princess cut diamond earrings a platform to be seen. A
thirty-two-inch platinum chain wrapped around her neck with a

charm that said KI sprayed in diamonds, rested between her visible cleavage. KI could tell
she had Roy's attention, as well as his guys' attention, from the way they were staring at her with lust in their eyes.

"Here you go, sweetie," the bartender said, handing KI her bottle. Going in the Birkin bag, she pulled out a knot of big faces and peeled off three of them and passed them to the bartender. Roy glanced at the knot of money and estimated the bank roll to be at least six stacks. He was intrigued by the diva before him. Roy made his move.

"Aye, lil mama, what's your name?" Roy asked, holding a bottle of Rémy.

"Well, it's definitely not, lil mama."

Roy smiled, showing the VVS diamonds in his grill. "My bad, beautiful. I'm out of line for tha corny ass spiel."

"You think?" KI replied with a take-along attitude.

"They call me Roy," Roy said, extending his hand in greeting. KI looked at his hand for a minute. He had enough ice on his fingers to freeze Africa.

"My name's Kiesha." KI shook his hand, smiling, showcasing her pearly whites.

"You here by yourself or you here with your nigga?"

"I'm here by myself and I don't have no nigga."

"Shit, as beautiful as you are, that's kind of hard to believe," Roy said, taking a swig from his bottle of Rémy.

"Well, believe it. I'm single because niggas in Chicago be on too much bullshit for me."

"You just fucking with the wrong niggas. You out here playing with these lil ass boys, when you can be fucking with a boss," Roy retorted, feeling himself from the liquor and pills he was off of.

"Is that right? You act like you know something I don't."

"Listen, baby…you with me for the night." Roy grabbed KI's hand and led her to the VIP, where he and his crew were poppin bottles and doing their thang. KI learned that Roy was from the westside of the city and had major influence over The Four Corner Hustlers, a violent drug crew that distributed heroin on the westside.

He was definitely a lick, so KI put Roy on The Homicide Crew's most-wanted list, and tonight would be the night they handled the bizness.

"So, what if the nigga get on some bullshit and don't want to tell us where the shit at?" Goon asked.

"Come on, my dude, stop acting like you new to this jack-boy shit. If that nigga get to playing, we gone get to spraying. We ain't playing no games about this shit. Straight up," Omega said, wishing Roy would buck so he could murk his ass, which he planned to do anyway.

"Man, we definitely ain't doing no faking with none of these weak ass niggas. We about to lay the streets down," Ace intervened, loading the thirty-shot extended magazine to his FN pistol. The Homicide Crew were all in a dangerous state of mind. They had already bonded their crime family by blood when they murdered the man in the gun store. Now armed with elite ammunition, loyalty and ambition, T.H.C. was ready to launch a deadly crime spree in the City of Chicago and tonight Roy would be the first blood sacrifice in the terror that was about to be unleashed in Chi-Raq.

"Y'all already know the drill when I send the text. We came out of the hotel. He is in a Bentley truck. Once y'all snatch him, I'm a jump in his whip and we gone meet back here."

"Say no more, my nigga," Omega replied, ready to activate. His adrenaline was rushing his motivation was fueled by balling out with his clique and standing ten toes down in the game of murder and drugs.

A half-hour later, KI stood on the porch of her mother's house. Roy was running a few minutes late. She was already agitated at the fact that she was going to have to give this weak ass nigga some pussy. She was starting to get sick, thinking about how she was setting her body out in order for The Homicide Crew to get close to their victims. After tonight, T.H.C. would have to come to the round table to come up with another route when putting in work.

KI was about to grab her cell phone to check Roy's whereabouts when her phone vibrated in her coat pocket. Glancing at her caller ID, she saw it was Roy, then she saw a dark-colored SUV turn the corner of her block. Roy had an expensive foreign whip, which pulled in front of her and parked at the curb. The windows were dark tinted, so you couldn't see who was in it. The twenty-six-inch Forgiatos had the truck sitting up nice.

KI made her way to the passenger side of the vehicle and was about to reach for the door, until it opened and a nigga climbed out. He was tall, about six foot three, with shoulder-length dreads covered by a black Chicago Bulls skull cap. He was dark complexioned and even though it was dark outside, the golf-ball-sized earrings on his earlobes were flooded with ice, shining. "What's good, lil mama? You can get in the front with our man," he said, getting in the backseat.

"Damn, I didn't know we were having a party," KI said, walking up to the truck but not getting in.

Roy smiled, showing the ice in his grill. "Nah baby, tonight about me and you. This my man's, Killa. I gotta drop him off at his car up north. Then we can go do us. You don't mind, do you?" KI took a second to think about it. If shit didn't pan out right and it looked like it was going to get sticky, the .40 ACP in her purse would get her out the jam, she was sure of it. She was a killer and she wouldn't hesitate to leave them a cold case. She got in the whip. The peanut butter leather interior seems to wrap her body like a glove. KI had never been inside a Bentley truck and she could now see why the SUV cost a quarter-mil. The smell of new high-grade marijuana and Roy's Burberry cologne engulfed the inside of the Bentley.

Roy pulled away from the curb as Lil Baby blasted through the factory speakers, grabbing the half-blunt of sour diesel Kush. He fired up the potent THC and inhaled the smoke in his lungs, before passing it to KI, who received it and took a pull. The loud was starting to put her in a hazy state but yet, she was still focused and on point.

After dropping his potna off, Ki and Roy had a nice little dinner at the Cheesecake Factory where they had shots of Patrón. The liquor and weed had them in a chill mode as Roy put all of his business on the table, trying to impress KI. The more info he gave up on his drug endeavors, the more she knew that in a matter of a couple of hours, she would be on and popping.

Pulling up into the parking lot of the extended stay on the north side of the city, Roy parked and hit the push button ignition and killed the engine. KI was a lil confused. They were supposed to be getting a room at the Congress downtown, now they were at the extended stay. "I'll be right back, shorty," Roy said before he hopped out the whip to go to pay for the room.

"Fuck!" KI cursed to herself. It seemed to her like everything was starting to go left. She started to abort the mission, but she had already come too far and invested too much time. "Fuck it." She sent a text to Omega, letting them know the location of the extended stay.

"Say no more," Omega texted back. KI put her phone back in her purse and grabbed the .40, pulling the slide back. She made sure a hollow point round was in the chamber and placed the weapon back in her handbag, just as Roy was walking back to the truck. He was stumbling, which let KI knew that he was definitely drunk. This was going to be like taking candy from a baby.

Once inside the luxurious suite, Roy plopped down on the king size bed. KI took her coat off and sat it on the chair.

"You mind if I take a shower real quick, boo?" KI said seductively, walking over to the bed where Roy was laying on his back.

"What do you need to take a shower for? Come over here and let a nigga get some of that pussy. I'ma lick you, clean anyway."

"Boy, you so nasty. But I like that nasty shit. Just let me go freshen up real quick and when I'm done, I'll come and take care of all of this," KI said, squeezing Roy's dick through his jeans. He almost bust a nut just from her touch.

"Hurry up, ma. I'm trying to dig all in that shit." KI made her way to the bathroom, putting an extra switch in her step. Roy watched lustfully while stroking his meat.

When KI got in the bathroom, she locked the door and turned the shower on. Pulling out her phone, she sent another text to Omega. "Where y'all niggas at?"

A minute later, Omega texted back. "We on Sheridan. We are about to pull up in about two minutes."

"Call my phone in exactly thirty minutes. Then we will be on our way out."

"Aight," was Omega's only reply. KI stripped down to just her boy shorts and matching lace bra. Going in her purse, she got some Mariah Carey perfume and applied a small amount on her wrists and rubbed them together. After folding her clothes neatly, she grabbed them and stepped out of the bathroom. Roy was laying on the bed almost half asleep when she walked out.

"Damn, nigga, I know you ain't about to fall asleep on a bitch?" Roy looked up to see KI walking towards him. Her ass was falling all out of her tight shorts, as her cleavage from her big ass titties was threatening to burst out from the confines of her bra. His dick began to swell ASAP.

"Shorty, you thick as fuck," he said stroking his pole. KI laughed slightly as she sat on the edge of the bed, removing Roy's hand from his dick and replacing it with her own.

"You got some more loud, baby? I'm trying to smoke."

Roy went in his pocket and pulled out what was left from the quarter-ounce he had copped earlier that day. "Grab them blunts from my jacket." KI stopped jacking his dick and went and got his leather Pelle Pelle jacket from off the chair. When she reached in the front part of the jacket, her manicured hand touched the plastic Glock that rested in the confines of the jacket. Now she knew Roy was strapped.

There was no way she could get back on the phone and text Omega. She didn't want to raise any suspicion. KI reached into his pocket and got the Garcia Vega's and went back over to the bed and told Roy to roll up. As he broke the cigar down, KI pulled Roy's Balmain jeans to his ankles.

"Your baby mama gone be mad at me for this one." KI pulled Roy's medium-sized dick from his boxer briefs and took all of him into her mouth. The warmth from her thick tongue caused a jolt to go through his body while he was breaking the Kush down inside the Garcia Vega, causing him to drop some of the loud on his chest.

"Ahh shit, girl!" KI had him moaning like he was the bitch as she went up and down on his love muscle. Roy managed to complete rolling the blunt of Kush and fired it up. KI stopped sucking on his dick to take a smoke break. While hitting the weed, Roy pulled one of her large breasts from her bra and took to it like a starving baby. The weed in her bloodstream and the way Roy was devouring her nipple made her pussy get wet. She was seriously thinking about letting Roy pound her pussy out, until her phone started to ring.

"Hold on, baby. I gotta get that," KI said with lust in her voice as she pushed Roy off her lightly. Grabbing her phone without looking at the caller ID, she answered.

"Hello? Wait… when? Oh my God! Mom, I'm on my way." She hung up the phone and made a dash for her clothes.

"What's wrong?" Roy asked, pulling up his boxer briefs.

"My daughter. She just spilled some hot grease on herself. I gotta go. You have to get me home," KI replied, visibly shaken as she began to dress.

"Damn, that's fucked up, shorty. Let's get up outta here." After they got dressed, KI and Roy made their way out the hotel and inside the Bentley Bentayga. Roy was about to pull out of his parking spot when all of a sudden, a black tinted Dodge Charger boxed him in and two masked men hopped out. Seeing the move, Roy reached in his jacket and pulled his Glock and cocked it, chambering a round.

"What, these niggaz think it's sweet, tryna jack me?" Roy sneered as he looked in his rearview mirror, watching the men advance on his truck.

"It's definitely sweet. Bitch ass nigga, drop tha hammer before I split your shit," KI said through clenched teeth, putting the .40 up under Roy's chin. He dropped his weapon, now coming to the terms that this fine ass bitch he was trying to fuck, had just set him up to get robbed. The driver's side of the Bentley was yanked open and Roy was forced at gunpoint out of his whip by a masked face that had his FN in Roy's face, point-blank range.

"Get yo bitch ass in the car, nigga," Goon said as he held Roy by the collar of his leather jacket, pushing him into the backseat of the Charger. Marcus climbed in the backseat with him, while Goon jumped into the driver's seat.

"I'll meet y'all back at the spot," KI yelled out the driver's side window of the truck. Goon put the Charger in reverse and pulled out the hotel's lot, with KI en route, back to the south side of the Chi. Roy sat in the backseat with a gun stuck to his ribs and a blindfold over his eyes. His heart was beating fast and the sweat poured from his forehead flowed profusely as the thought of his own death clouded his thoughts. He had done a lot in the streets to get the position he had on the west side. Now he was wondering whether it was all worth it.

CHAPTER 5

YaYo had just finished doing his push-up routine that consisted of doing fifty push-ups. "Forty-nine, forty-eight..." He'd counted all the way down to one. He had to keep his mind off of the jail house murder he had committed. It had been two days since the incident in C-1 with the Alabama inmates. After S.I.S. reviewed the video footage of that day, the prison administration was able to recapture the assault and in return, they headed to C-1 to get the rest of the inmates that were involved in the violence. B.D. Pook and Harold were also picked up and were now cellies on Range 3, awaiting disciplinary shots for the assault. YaYo grabbed his washcloth to wipe the sweat from his face.

"How many do you do?" G-Wayne asked as he sat on his bunk reading a book called a Shooter's Ambition: Birth of a Sniper by an urban author named S. Allen.

"I did fifty down on the push-ups."

"Damn, Blood. That's like twelve hunnid and fifty push-ups."

"Yeah, I know. I normally do that shit in like an hour and a half. I fell off a lil bit. Me and Latin Folks '3' used to do this shit all the time," YaYo replied.

YaYo had just finished showering in the small shower inside the two-man cell when two C.O.'s came to the cell and opened the food slot. "Yaton Anderson, we are going to ask you to stick your hands out of the slot, so we can cuff you up. The captain wants to have a word with you," the C.O. said, taking a pair of handcuffs off his utility belt.

Man, what the fuck these crackers want with me? YaYo thought as he stuck his hands out of the slot. The correctional officers placed YaYo in cuffs and double-checked them to make sure they were locked. Grabbing his walkie talkie, he said, "Range 3, cell 42, open up." A few seconds later, YaYo's cell door opened and the C.O. grabbed him by his cuffs and led him out of the cell. "Range 3 cell 42, close it up." The cell door closed. The C.O.'s led YaYo down the steps and to the captain's office. When he got to the office, Captain Dunbar sat at his desk and on the opposite side of the oakwood desk, sat S.I.S. Lieutenant Crab with a disgusted look on his face.

"Y'all can leave him here. We'll make sure we return him to his cell." S.I.S. Crab started standing up. The two C.O.'s left out the captain's office and closed the door behind them.

"Well, well, well. Mr. Gang Leader Yaton Anderson, aka YaYo. I got some good news and I got some bad news. Which one do you want to hear first, gangsta?" S.I.S. Crab asked sarcastically. YaYo smirked in his face but remained silent.

"Yeah, I got it, Mr. I'm a Stand-Up Dude, but let me tell you this, cocksucka, they were able to bring that inmate back to life." S.I.S Crab studied YaYo's facial expression closely, trying to mentally read him, which was close to impossible. Even though a huge weight had just been lifted off YaYo's shoulder, he wouldn't let Crab see it. YaYo had mastered the art of not wearing his emotions on your sleeve.

"You know, I just recently went over your P.S.I. and after reading it, I can surely see why the courts recommended you to be designated here. USP Pollock is a level-7 penitentiary, which means we house the worst of the worst criminals in the country. Most of the inmates on this compound have so much time that nine out of ten, they will grow old and die here. But guess what, asshole? This is not the worst situation you can be in. You do know that, don't you?" YaYo continued to stay in control, even though he wanted nothing more than to break S.I.S. Crab's jaw. The captain started shuffling through some papers in front of him.

"Mr. Anderson, we have just gotten word from our superiors up at Grand Prairie who have just recommended that you be transferred and designated to the S.M.U. program." At the sound of S.M.U. Program, YaYo diverted his attention to Captain Dunbar. YaYo knew very well what the S.M.U. program was. The S.M.U. stood for a Special Management Unit and was located in Lewisburg, Pennsylvania. The S.M.U. was an eighteen-month program. Inmates sent to Lewisburg were sent on disciplinary transfer for serious violations committed on B.O.P. grounds. Most inmates were sent to the S.M.U. for stabbings, staff assaults, drug possession to murder.

The S.M.U. program was twenty-three hours a day locked down, three showers a week, no visit or telephone usage was available, depending on what phase you were in the program. The first phase was a fifteen-minute phone call, the second phase of the program was two fifteen-minute calls, the third phase was four fifteen-minute calls and the last phase was adjustment for transfer back to a regular USP institution, so normal phone privileges were given back to the inmate.

The S.M.U. program was designed to break the hardest of men in the federal system. The living conditions in Lewisburg was unbearable. In the summer it would get so hot, due to no ventilation in the hundred-year-old prison that all you could do in the small cell was just lay there and sweat. The winter was the total opposite. The inmates would have to literally have on every piece of clothing the administration provided, in order to stay slightly warm. Lewisburg Penitentiary was hell on earth and the C.O.'s that worked in USP Lewisburg made sure all the inmates felt the harsh conditions and knew who was in charge—the C.O.'s.

"Mr. Anderson, you will have a S.M.U. hearing in four months from today for an evaluation, which to me is a waste of time and taxpayers' money. But, it's protocol for your admission into the program. Here is a copy of your disciplinary shot. Read it and sign right here, saying that you received a copy." Captain Dunbar handed YaYo the shot, which he grabbed with handcuffed hands.

YaYo read the shot that said:

You have a history of serious and disruptive disciplinary infractions. Additionally, you participated in misconduct that adversely affected the orderly operation at a correctional facility. Specifically, on September 9, 2018, inmates associated with the security threat groups, Black Gangster Disciples and Folks Nation, assaulted inmates from the geographical area of Alabama over a disrespect issue. You and others began assaulting inmates from the geographical area of Alabama.

Upon observation, one inmate struck another inmate associated with the Folks Nation, then joined the assault. You were observed on recorded video surveillance, stabbing another inmate in a striking motion. The inmate suffered three critical puncture wounds, one to the kidney, one in the chest and one in the inmate's left lung, causing his lung to collapse from the blunt trauma. The inmate was taken off the compound and rushed to the hospital by Med-Flight.

You will be provided the opportunity to appear at the hearing. The hearing administrator will determine whether you appear at the hearing via video conference, telephone conference, or in person at your current facility.

"Man, how y'all gonna serve me this bogus ass shot?" YaYo asked, speaking for the first time. He read the shot, knowing it was bogus as hell as the incident didn't go as they wrote it. He knew they were sending him to the S.M.U. being biased. They were mad because the Alabama cat survived, and they couldn't give YaYo any more time.

"Just sign the fucking shot saying you received it, asshole, so we can get you back to your little cell," Crab said, emphasizing the word little. YaYo signed the disciplinary shot.

"Now, Mr. Anderson, when you get to Lewisburg, make sure you get in a cell with one of your homeboys, or it might not end up good for you. You know, it's a lot of D.C. cats down there," the captain said, laughing.

The administration knew D.C. inmates were always a problem and they hated niggas from the Midwest. Mostly Chicago inmates, because they were part of a gang culture, a culture D.C. cats despised. The federal system was full of D.C. inmates, because the District of Columbia didn't have a state prison, so all niggas in D.C. that was charged and convicted of a crime were sent up there.

After signing his shot, S.I.S. Crab escorted YaYo back to his cell. "You know, Anderson, I don't think you're ever going to make it out the feds. Lewisburg is a different breed and I'm quite sure your gangbanging homies will send you off to do some stupid shit that get you re-indicted," Crab said, standing with YaYo in front of his cell, waiting for the officer at the control booth to pop YaYo's cell.

"Fuck you!" YaYo said through clenched teeth.

"No, fuck you. You might get more pussy that way. Pop Cell 42," Crab spoke into the walkie talkie. YaYo's door opened. "Step in the cell, tough guy." After YaYo was secured inside the confines of his cell, YaYo noticed his celly G-Wayne was in the bunk with the sheet over his head.

"They did mail while you were gone, Blood. I put your mail on your bed," G-Wayne said from under the covers.

"Good looking, fam." YaYo looked at his bunk and saw the envelope. YaYo grabbed the mail. Looking at the name and address of one envelope, he thought he had the wrong mail at first, until he saw it contained some pictures and a letter. He looked through the pictures first. The first picture he saw was of a smiling little boy who seemed to be mixed. He had a full head of curly black hair and his facial features were very familiar. At least six of the pictures were of the cute little boy. The other picture was of the body of some female from the neck down. She was short and thick. *Who the fuck is this?* YaYo thought.

He kept going through the pics until he came up on one where the female was posing from the back. She wore a black Victoria's Secret thong that was stuck between her meaty, thick ass cheeks. A funny-shaped birthmark was on her ass. On the streets, he had sexed a lot of different women. Not only did the dope game bring money, it also brought women. YaYo would never pinpoint the birthmark to a name. Whoever it was, was trying to withhold their identity by not revealing their face. And that was weird, so he thought. YaYo then read the letter in the envelope that smelled of a fruity fragrance. He opened the letter.

"Dear Yaton, I hope this letter reaches you in good spirit as well as health. I know you are sitting somewhere confused by this, but I promise by the end of this letter, you will have this completely figured out. First and foremost, I want to say that I truly miss you. I have feelings for you, Yayo. Feelings that I never would've thought would come over me. It has been a little over a year since I last saw you. A year since you had my mind and body captivated for that quick fifteen minutes." YaYo arched his eyebrow in confusion as he continued to read.

"When I found out I was pregnant with Jamari, I didn't know what to do. I didn't want to bring him into this cold world without a father, so I was going to abort my pregnancy. But when I got on that cold table, I couldn't proceed and go through with it. I want a family with you, Yaton. I know what I want in life. And it's you, baby. Then I heard the best news in my life. When I heard they reversed your sentence, that let me know I had made the right choice. All I want you to know is that we are waiting on you to come home. By now, you should have put this together. The address on the envelope is the address you can reach me at. If you need anything, I mean anything, let me know. We miss and love you. Always, your baby momma."

YaYo dropped the letter on the floor. He couldn't believe what he had just read. YaYo reread the part when she said, "It has been over a year since I last saw you. A year since you had my mind and body captivated for that quick fifteen minutes." Looking at the picture again, he knew at that moment who the sexy body belonged to. A smile plastered across his face as he spoke her name. "C.O. Sanchez."

It was as if she just disappeared. YaYo had asked around and through inmate-gossip.com he had learned that C.O. Sanczhez was transferred to Pollock F.C.I. to work at medium security for the rest of the yearly quarter. Now her change of demeanor made sense to him. She found out she was pregnant with his seed and didn't know what to do. YaYo went back to the picture of the little boy. He stared at the picture, focusing on the baby's facial features and then knew why Jamari looked so familiar to him. It was because Jamari looked almost identical to Shamira when she was born. YaYo knew by looking at the little boy in the picture that he was definitely his son.

YaYo shook his head from his newfound news. His emotions were running wild. He was happy he had a son in the world, as he always wanted a boy, offspring to carry on his name, but at the same time he was scared. What was he going to tell Shakira? Him having a baby on her would break their trust. How was he going to tell the mother of his child that he had gotten another woman pregnant while he was incarcerated? Skakira would definitely be crushed and the chances of her staying with him was slim to none, but it was impossible to keep his son a secret, as he would have to come clean sooner or later if he ever wanted to be part of Jamari's life. YaYo grabbed the letter, folded it and put it back in the envelope, along with the pictures, and put the envelope under his mattress.

Today, YaYo had received major news that forever changed his life. First, he found out the Alabama nigga he stabbed up in C-1 had made it through, so the chances of YaYo getting re-indicted on a jailhouse body was now nonexistent. There was a saying that stated, "God looks after babies, and fools." YaYo didn't know what category he fell in, but he knew Allah had given him a blessing. Then to find out he had a son somewhere out there in the world, shocked him.

YaYo had a lot going on in his life right now and to top it all off, he was about to be shipped to Lewisburg, Pennsylvania, where he would have to endure serious living conditions, as his communication would be very limited to the outside world. For a hundred and eighty months. He would be leaving USP Pollock, but the thing that would hurt him the most was that he would be leaving Mr. B, a man who had become l his mentor as well as a father figure. The thought alone had him vexed.

Honey, YaYo's grandmother, once told him, "God will put people in your life for a reason." YaYo didn't know where his life was going at the minute. All he could do now is just take it day by day and hope whatever God's plan for him was a blessing, instead of a curse.

CHAPTER 6

Slap!

The open palm connecting with Roy's jaw stung for the impact of the blow, causing his eyes to water. He was bound to a chair, naked as the day he was born, inside the dimly lit basement at the trap spot on Bishop. Omega, Ace, Goon, Marcus and KI stood around him, waiting for him to come out of his slight coma. Marcus had repeatedly pistol-whipped Roy all the way to the south side as he occupied the backseat with Roy. The Homicide Crew were all eager to get the location of Roy's drugs and money.

"Now, let's pick back up to where we were before you took your lil nap," Omega said.

"Ma, look. I don't know what y'all talking 'bout. Y'all got my money already," Roy retorted. KI had gotten eight gees out his pocket and his black card. She also had the Bentley truck that they were going to take to the chop shop first thing in the a.m. Roy spit out one of his loose front teeth. His lips were swollen and looked like a duck's mouth, both eyes were swollen shut and yet he still wanted to play childish games. KI walked over and sat her thick ass cheeks on his blood soiled jeans.

"Listen boo, now is not the time to be playing around. You was talking all that big baller shit. 'Me and my niggas got the west side on lock. I'm a boss.' Now don't tell me you was doing all that faking," KI retorted, mimicking Roy when he was trying to impress her. Roy looked at KI with pure hatred, before he spit blood in her face. KI slapped him with the butt of her .40 Glock.

"Bitch ass nigga!" She sneered as she watched the blood drip down the side of his face from the freshly inflicted wound caused by her Glock.

"Aye, Joe! This nigga playing. Goon, hand me that rod real quick." Goon walked over and grabbed a black pole, called a cattle prod. It was used to move a herd of cows. By touching the cow with the cattle prod, the prod would release about two hundred and twenty volts of electricity into the cow, thus making the cow move somewhere. Ace had seen the cattle prod used on a cow on the Discovery Channel and the wheels in his brain started to turn. If two hundred and twenty volts would make a big ass cow move, it would surely make a dope boy tell where his stash was located. Ace grabbed the cattle prod from Goon, slipping it inside his right palm, walking over to Roy.

"Now listen, pussy. If you don't want to die, tell us what we want to hear. You can tell us where the shit at or we can search for it. We already know where you lay your head at, my nigga," Ace lied.

"I already told y'all, that's all I got."

"So, you really want us to search for this lil shit, huh? Just know if we gotta search for it, it's gone be on your dead body," Ace replied as he touched Roy's nut-sack with the cattle prod, causing two hundred and twenty volts of electricity to dance through his body. Ace held it there for a few seconds. Roy's body stiffened as his eyes rolled to the back of his head, it felt as if he had been struck by lightning. Ace took the prod off his nuts.

"Where the fuck is the money and drugs?

"Please y'all, don't kill me. Please," Roy pleaded.

"Wrong answer." Ace put the prod back on his private parts, but this time with more force than before.

"Ahhhh," Roy yelled in agony, smoke coming from his mouth from being electrocuted. The basement smelled of burnt hair and shit, from Roy losing his bowels. Ace took the prod off again.

"Last time, fam. Where the work?" Roy could hardly respond, he was in pain and he knew the niggas before him would kill him, depending on the next words that came out of his mouth.

"Okay, God dammit. Ok," Roy screamed, not wanting to feel the cattle prod again.

"That's what I want to hear."

Visibly scared and in pain, Roy stuttered, "It-it's a house on 41st and Prairie, 4102 South Prairie. It's a safe upstairs in the bathroom closet in the corner."

"What's the combination?" KI sneered with murder in her eyes.

"It's-it's all in the safe. The money and dope," Roy confessed. KI stored the address and the combination to the safe inside her iPhone.

"Goon, you come with me. Omega, Ace and Marcus, y'all stay here with this nigga. If everything, everything I'm a let y'all know," KI commanded and grabbed Roy's keys and left the trap.

Thirty minutes later, KI and Goon pulled up in front of a house on 41st and Prairie. KI pulled her hoodie over her head and double checked her .40 to make sure a hollow point round occupied the weapon's barrel. Goon did the same. If these was any waiting surprises, he was going to air that shit out. Period. It was dark outside, and the block was quiet as the two thugs slid out Roy's Bentley truck, with guns clutched on their waistlines.

Once on the front porch of the house, KI pulled out Roy's keys in an attempt to directly open up the door. Goon stood on guard with his hammer out. The lights in the house was off, indicating that nobody was home. Sticking the key into the lock mechanism, she turned the key and the door opened. KI extended her weapon in front of her, holding the combat firearm with both hands as if she was trained to carry it. Goon slid in behind her, closing the front door once he entered.

The house was dark except from the rays of the streetlight that was beaming inside of the house. KI nodded her head towards the staircase and led the way up the stairs to the second floor of the home. Finding the bathroom, they were looking for KI flicked the light switch on the wall only to see plenty of huge roaches scattering to safety. Goon stood outside the bathroom as security with his gun out.

Walking to the small closet, KI moved some dirty clothes out the way, and staring her in her face was a medium-sized safe in the corner of the closet. Kneeling down, she pulled out her iPhone and found the combination she had saved in her phone. Putting the combination into the electronic keypad, the safe popped open.

The contents inside the safe made KI's pussy moist as she stared at six neatly wrapped kilos of heroin and about thirteen stacked bundles of cash. KI quickly pulled the Glad garbage bag from the small of her back and proceeded to fill it with the drugs and money. Slinging the load over her back, she rushed out the filthy bathroom. Tapping Goon on the way out, signaling for him. "Let's bounce."

Back inside the basement on Bishop, Roy was still feeling like he was on the TV show *Naked and Afraid*, his head hurt like hell and his feet felt as if they had gotten frostbite in the freezing basement. He had mentally vowed that if he made it out of this situation alive, he was going to murder everyone involved.

Omega was breaking down a Swisher Sweet to roll his fourth blunt, until his phone vibrated in his pocket, looking at his phone he read the text from KI that said, "Everything is everything. Handle that." Omega smiled and put the phone back in his pocket and finished rolling the weed. They fired it up and took a strong pull. Blowing the smoke out through his nostrils, he turned his attention to Ace and Marcus.

"That was KI just a minute ago."

"What she saying? What's the bizness, my nigga?" Ace asked, full of adrenaline. Omega took another strong pull off the blunt, before passing it to Ace.

"She said everything all well," he replied.

"So, what we gone do with this nigga?"

"Playa right here was an asset. Now, he's just a liability," Omega replied before pulling his pistol out.

"Man, I gave y'all the information y'all needed. Come on, let me go. I promise, you niggas a never hear from me again." Tears rolled down Roy's face as he knew he was about to die.

"Let me holler at you two niggas right quick." Omega gestured towards Ace and Marcus. The three of them walked into the far corner of the basement. "Now, this is the business. We all know buddy got to go. The question is, who want to do it?" Marcus put his head down.

"Nigga, what difference do it make? Let's just bust this nigga so we can get the fuck up outta here," Ace replied, taking his gun off his hip.

"Nah, it does make a difference. You know, Marcus, you've been around the squad for a minute. Don't you think it's time for you to make your bones amongst T.H.C.?" Marcus was definitely a thug that played the games of the street, but since rotating with T.H.C., his criminal activities had become more extensive as the whole crew was involved in the streets something heavy. Being a part of their gang put Marcus on another level.

Not wanting to seem soft in front of his potna's, he grabbed the strap from off the counter and walked over to Roy, who was shaking like a crap game and scared to death. Taking the initiative, he raised the gun to Roy's head with his finger resting firmly on the trigger. His heart was beating fast, knowing he was about to end the life of another human being. He had to go through with it. If he didn't, he would be looked at as pure pussy and knowing his two psychotic homies, they would turn on him and add his body to Chicago's already high murder rate.

Marcus closed his eyes and pulled the trigger. The slight recoil from the weapon caused the gun to jerk inside the palm of his hand. The gunshot was thunderous inside the small confined basement, causing his ears to ring. The strong smell of copper invaded the air waves. Opening his eyes, he saw Roy with a large hole in the center of his head. A red jelly-like goo escaped from the hole along with a chunky bloody matter. Marcus threw up from the sight and smell of death.

"Come on, my nigga. Let's get the fuck up outta here," Ace said, bringing Marcus out of the shock of catching his first body. Omega smiled as he watched Roy's brains leak to the floor. He was a cold-blooded killa that understood murder. He knew that to kill another man and get away with it was a euphoria that was better than ecstasy. If today was Marcus's first body, he knew that Marcus would kill again, as the homicide would become his addiction, turning him into a complete savage.

After leaving Roy's body in the basement dead as a doorknob, Omega, Ace and Marcus left the trap. Setting it on fire before they left, leaving no evidence they got en route to get up with KI and Goon, who had gotten Roy's stash. They had put in the work and now it was time to relish in the fruits of their labor.

CHAPTER 7

Rockett and Choppa sat lowkey in a black tinted Maserati Levante in front of the Berry Homes Projects in North Memphis. They had been in Memphis, trying to catch up with Breed and Roscoe, who had been ducking their calls with much disrespect. Quavon felt they were trying to cut ties with the G.B.C., because they had another cocaine and heroin plug. Quavon and the G.B.C. made a lot of money in Memphis, dealing with the two hustla's and them copping work from another source was something he didn't want to endure, so he sent these designated hitters to Memphis to try and get some kind of understanding.

"So, you mean to tell me we gotta holler at these niggas first?" Choppa asked sunk low in the passenger seat. His White Sox fitted cap tilted to the right, slightly covering his eyes.

"Yup," Rockett replied from the driver's seat.

"My nigga, I don't see the sense of all this politicking. This shit ain't no democracy. It's a dictatorship. Either they get the work from G.B.C., or they lay the fuck down. This shit ain't that hard. This shit elementary." Choppa was ready to put in work.

"Fuck is these niggas at, shawty?" Rockett said to himself glancing at his Richard Mille timepiece that read 9:45. Even though it was a little late, the Berry Homes Projects were in full swing on this hot August night. Crowds of people hung out smoking, drinking, playing spades or doing whatever else black folks do in the hood in the summer. Rockett was just about to start to get agitated until a cocaine-white BMW X5 pulled into the parking lot and parked three cars down from the G.B.C.

A tall, skinny cat with shoulder-length dreadlocks, stepped out the passenger seat with a bag full of Popeye's Chicken. He was dressed in dark blue linen shorts, a matching linen Polo, and a pair of midnight blue New Balances adorned his feet. The driver of the vehicle got out with his cell phone glued to his ear. He was bald-headed and wearing all black. His jewels shined from the light coming from the streetlights in the parking lot.

"Here go these clown ass niggas right here. Watch this," Rockett said, grabbing his cell phone and dialing a number. Breed and Roscoe were walking past a clique of hood rats when Roscoe's phone rang. Looking at the caller ID, he saw it was Rockett's number and answered.

"What's up?" he answered rudely.

"What's good, shawty? This your boy, Rockett, loc."

"I know who the fuck this is. What's good, playboy, because time—especially my time—is worth money," Roscoe said, arrogant as hell.

"Listen, shawty, I got a message from Quavon."

"Oh yeah? I'm listening."

"My nigga say y'all been doing good business and he feel like the feelings ain't mutual."

"Fuck his feelings. You right, *we* been doing good business. This nigga steady trying to bird feed us. Nigga trying to rise, not be stagnated," Roscoe retorted as him and Breed entered the trap inside Berry Homes Projects.

"Yes, we figured you could say that, but we wanna continue the business. We goin up the shipment on your consignment. it's going to be the same work and the prices gone remain the same." There was faint laughter and then silence, Roscoe had disconnected the call.

"Who the fuck was that?" Breed asked, sitting his keys on the counter.

"That was them Chicago niggas, talking about they gone flood us with more bricks, but they gone keep the price tag the same. Them niggas got to be smoking dope or some shit, thinking we finna keep hustling for them. Suge flooding us, the work better and his price better. Fuck them G.B.C. niggas. And if they want some smoke, we with that shit too," Rosco vented. He never really liked Rockett anyway, he just dealt with him because he had a line on some coke.

When he was introduced to Suge on Bill Street at a bar by a mutual acquaintance, the stage had been set for Breed and Roscoe to make some major money and that's what they were going to continue to keep doing. The G.B.C. was just a stepping-stone for them until they came up with a better plug. Breed and Roscoe wasn't loyal to the G.B.C. Their loyalty was to each other.

"So, we just gone say fuck them?" Breed asked as he went into the kitchen to grab some Vision cookware, filling half of the Pyrex with lukewarm water. Breed placed it on the Kenmore stove and turned the eye on, while Roscoe took half a kilo out of the Popeye's Chicken bag.

"That's exactly what we gone say. Fuck them. We don't need them and we definitely don't owe them shit," Roscoe replied, giving Breed the half-brick. The two hustlers proceeded to cook the drugs and bag up the work, getting ready to flood the crack spots with work. The night was still young and their hustla state of mind had them in grind mode.

Click Clack! was the sound of a hollow point bullet being chambered in the barrel of Rockett's .45 Caliber XDM. It had been three hours since Breed and Roscoe had pulled inside the Berry Homes and they were waiting for them to come out.

"Fam, let's just go in there, kick the door in and let it do what it do," Choppa said from the passenger seat, screwing a silencer on his P-89 Ruger.

"Just chill, shawty, I got this shit." Rockett pulled the black ski mask over his face, concealing his identity. The crowd had thinned out as nobody but fiends roamed the project grounds. Roscoe covered his head with his Polo hoodie.

"Aye, shawty. I'm a go set the alarm off in they whip. Whoever come downstairs, we gone hit him. Then we going to go upstairs and smoke the other nigga. You feel me?"

"Say no more," was Choppa's only reply as Rockett slid out the car. Walking over to the BMW X5, Rockett kicked the passenger side door, thus activating the alarm before he briskly walked back to his vehicle and got in the driver's seat.

"Now we wait," Rockett said, placing his gun on his lap.

Breed was in the process of breaking up some crack to be bagged up when the key chain to the X5 began to vibrate, indicating the alarm was going off. Getting up from the task at hand, Breed looked out the window down at the parking lot and saw the head-lights of the Beamer truck blinking on and off. Sticking his keychain out the window, he hit the button to silence the alarm.

"Got damn. Weak ass alarm," he said, frustrated that he was apparently out of range to turn off the alarm. Now he had to go downstairs. He wasn't really trippin, he had to go get the blunts from out the glove box anyway, so he set out on his mission.

"Look alive, shawty, look like we got some action," Rockett spoke, noticing Breed's shadowy figure walking toward the SUV. Choppa grabbed the door handle and was attempting to get out until Rockett grabbed him by the arm. "Hold up. We do him when he's on the way back." The two killas watched intensely as Breed opened the passenger side door and retrieved something, then was making his way back.

"Now," was Rockett's words before he calmly slid out the driv-er's seat. Choppa did the same. Breed was totally off focus until he heard the footsteps coming from behind him. But by this time, it was a little too late. When he turned around, he met face-to-face with the barrel of Choppa's Ruger.

"Quavon said it's either get down or lay down, and since you don't want to get down, then pussy lay down," Choppa hissed after squeezing the trigger once. *Psssst*! The slug hit Breed in his face, pushing his brains out his hat rack. His body dropped to the pave-ment right after the hot shells littered the concrete.

"Fuck his goofy ass leave the front door open for?" Roscoe said to himself, wondering why Breed left the door wide open. Roscoe was closing the door until it was violently kicked in. The door smashed his face, breaking his nose in the process. Rockett and Choppa rushed inside the small apartment with semi-autos drawn. Roscoe stood in shock as blood poured from his wound profusely.

"Talk that gangsta shit now, shawty." Rockett aimed his weapon at Roscoe and without even blinking, shot Roscoe at point-blank range in the head and chest, ending his young life. After shooting Roscoe ten times with the .45, Rockett released Roscoe of his Sprint iPhone and made his way out the apartment. A small crowd had started to hover over Breed's soulless body as it lay sprawled out in the parking lot. Rockett and Choppa discreetly got back into the Maserati and pulled out of the Berry Homes Projects with a double murder added to their massive body count.

Quavon was at peak power as his goal and ambition was to be the most feared crime boss in the United States of America. YaYo had left the streets a certified hood legend. Quavon wanted to exceed YaYo's stats. When he left the game, whether it be from the guns in his enemies' clutches, or the United States government, his name would be spoken for years to come. He had the connections and the shooters to keep him at the top of the pyramid. He would forever and always be remembered as a chief of the G.B.C.

S. Allen

CHAPTER 8

"Shamira, can you please hurry up? We are running late," Shakira yelled upstairs to her five-year-old daughter. She had thirty minutes to be at work at the beauty salon and she had to drop Shamira off at her grandmother Karen's house before she went to work.

"I'm coming, Mama!" she screamed from her room as she tried to decide if she was going to wear her pink and white Jordan Retro 4's or her all-white K-Swiss low tops. Deciding on her Jordan's, she put them on and tied them and made her way downstairs, where her mother waited impatiently with her overnight bag.

"I'm ready, Mama."

"It's about time, here." Shakira handed Shamira her book bag that contained a change of clothes, toothbrush, lotion and other toiletries she would need while at her grandmother's house.

Once inside the car, Shamir put on her seat belt. She was happy she was spending a night at Grandma Karen's. Shamira loved her grandmother as she always showered with Karen's love. They would bake cookies, watch scary movies and Karen would read to her. The best part of the visits was when Karen would talk about their father. At her young age, Shamira was starting to be intrigued by the knowledge of her father. Shamira was almost a spitting image of YaYo. They bore the same skin complexion, same smile and facial features, as well as his quick temper.

Shamira knew her dad was in prison but was too young to understand what prison really was. She had asked Shakira countless times what her father was in prison for and Shakira would reply with the same answer. "Baby, because he made a bad mistake. But everybody makes mistakes."

"When will my daddy be coming home, Mama?" Shamira would then ask. She was anxious for her father to come home, as she had gotten accustomed to monthly visits and phone calls as the relationship they were building was becoming stronger and stronger.

"He will be home soon, baby."

"When, Mama?"

"When you turn eight years old, honey. Your daddy will be home," Shakira would tell her daughter.

Shakira pulled into the driveway of Karen's condo in the Rogers Park area on the north side of the city.

"Now you be good for Grandma and Mommy will be here in the morning to pick you up, okay?" Shakira said, turning to face her little princess as Karen stood at her doorway patiently waiting.

"Okay, Mama, I will... and I love you," Shamira replied before kissing her mother and getting out of the car.

Shakira honked the horn and waved at her mom, who returned with a wave of her own. Shakira was pulling out of the driveway when Shamira stopped in stride and started back running toward the car, waving her hands in the air to get her mother's attention. Shakira stopped the car, seeing her daughter running towards her. Parking, she got out the car.

"What is it, Shamira? I told you I was running late for work."

"Mama, I forgot. If my daddy call, can you please tell him that I love and miss him?" Shakira grabbed her chest as the words spoken from her daughter caused a slight pain in her heart. Her daughter was getting older and starting to feel the effects of not having her father, and it hurt her to the core. She couldn't wait for her child's father to come home so he could fill the void in both of their lives.

"Don't worry, baby. When he calls, I will surely give him your message. Okay, sweetie?'

"Thank you, Mama," Shamira said, before she ran back over towards her grandmother. Shakira got back in her car and pulled off just as a tear fell from her eye. She needed YaYo home like yesterday She was doing all she could to stay strong and keep their family together, but it was times like these that she felt weak, and needed YaYo's touch or words of love and he was down to help keep her together.

She hadn't heard from him in over a week, so she took it upon herself to call the prison to see if YaYo was okay. The administration told her YaYo was in the hole for an incident he was directly involved in that happened on the compound, and that he would soon be transferred to another correctional facility. When and where was information that was being withheld for security purposes.

All Shakira could do was wait for her baby daddy to contact her and let her know what the business was. She already knew he was a gangsta and was also trained to go. She just hoped and prayed he was safe and in good well-being.

Shakira pulled up in front of the Style and Grace Beauty Salon almost fifteen minutes late. Even though it was Karen's shop, she was always taught to lead by example, so she always wanted to be sharp and focused on time, to show the other stylists how to go by the mission statement at Style and Grace. Walking in the shop, she saw everybody was there as the chairs were all full, except hers.

"My bad, Bianca. I know I'm a little late. I had to drop Shamira off at Karen's," Shakira explained to one of her regulars that had been patiently waiting for her to arrive, so she could get her hair permed. Shakira walked over to her station to set things up. After she was good and ready, she told Bianca to come and have a seat in her chair. Bianca came into the shop once a week and was also a good friend of Shakira's. Shakira was doing her hair as Bianca read the *Chicago Tribune.*

"Girl, they mess around and let Larry Hoover out the feds," Bianca said, looking at the newspaper.

"Who is Larry Hoover?" Shakira asked, using a straight comb to press Bianca's shoulder-length, natural hair.

"Girl, you don't know who Mr. Hoover is? He started the Gangster Disciples back in the day. He was always speaking about growth and development and building the community up," Bianca informed.

"Well, how did he end up in the feds?"

"I really don't know. I guess he was becoming too powerful for these crackers and had much influence. It says here that his wife is suing the feds."

"Read the article out loud, girl," Shakira said, now thinking about her baby daddy. Every time somebody mentioned the feds or penitentiary, her thoughts were consumed with thoughts of YaYo.

Bianca began to read. "Notorious former leader of the Gangster Disciples, Larry Hoover, is suing ADX Florence which has been described as the 'Worst Prison in the world,' because he and his partner claim the prison has intentionally isolated him from his family. Winndye Jenkins held her Batman-costumed, five-year-old grandson's hand, guiding him through canopies of metal detectors and heavily armed prison guards. They were at United States Penitentiary ADX Florence, to visit his grandfather and her longtime partner, Larry Hoover, the notorious former leader of the Chicago gang, the Gangster Disciples.

Hoover transformed the Gangster Disciples into a community group called 'Growth and Development,' which focused on making positive gains in the Chicago Black community, such as education, entrepreneurship, and wellness. Prison officials and prosecutors interpreted his attempts as subversive, criminally genius, and a disingenuous way for him to remain leader of the Gangster Disciples while lying his way to possible clemency. But many of Hoover's supporters say his community work is vital and genuine, and that Hoover is a political prisoner.

That was eleven years ago, but Jenkins is used to having things taken away every time they come from Chicago to the breath-snatching attitudes of Florence, Colorado. The family's visitation is revoked often, for arbitrary reasons or genuine human error. Once it was her teenage granddaughter's cell phone accidentally left in her pocket, casting the whole family visitation rights for a year even though the family turned the phone in themselves when she realized it.

Hoover's very presence in ADX, rather than another, less-restricted prison, causes indignation among many of his supporters, who have argued that Hoover's leadership was critical to maintaining order in the streets of Chicago. It's important to note that in addition to Hoover, ADX Florence also imprisons several high-ranking Al-Qaeda. Many Muslim men at the prison, held on terrorism charges, were tortuously force-fed when they attempted to go on a hunger strike. Knowing her partner will never escape this place is impossibly hard for Jenkins to tolerate, but she keeps going on.

Jenkins has lived most of her life loving Larry though a glass, through the brutal intermediaries of metal detectors and fences, and phones and guards, as well as inspections and visitation termination. For Jenkins, this lawsuit is about fighting for her family's dignity. It's about making sure Hoover isn't isolated from the love and support of his family and loved ones. It's about resisting dehumanization and affirming her family's right to be a family and communicate with each other." Bianca finished reading and Shakira was in shock as she listened to Bianca read the article on Larry Hoover.

"Damn girl, that's fucked up how they are doing the man. The feds be on some straight bullshit," Bianca said, turning the page, now reading the local section of the paper. Shakira's heart went out to Larry Hoover and his wife, Winndye Jenkins. She could very well relate to what Winndye was going through as she remembered the countless times she flew to Louisiana, only to find out the prison was on lockdown status due to violence. Before YaYo had been sent to prison with a life sentence, their once strong bond had been diluted, due to the mental strain on their relationship, causing Shakira to fall weak and almost let TB break up their family.

After listening to Bianca read the article on Larry Hoover and Winndye Jenkins, Shakira now saw the strength in Ms. Jenkins for her husband and her undying loyalty, and that alone gave Shakira a boost of morale to overcome what her family was going through. She had to be strong, not just for herself, but for YaYo and Shamira. It would be up to her to be the glue that kept her family bonded together.

Shakira began to think. Whoever Winndye Jenkins was, she was definitely a special person that she wouldn't mind meeting.

"What's that lady name again. His wife?" Shakira asked.

"Her name is Winndye Jenkins. Why?"

"I'll see if I can reach her on Facebook, I want to speak to her. Find out what's her secret on staying so focused. You know?"

"Yeah girl, I feel you. Lil mama is for sho a ridah," Bianca responded.

"So, what else in the paper?" Shakira asked, putting Bianca's hair in a wrap.

"You already know. Chicago is so messed up. It's too much death in this city. They say the murder rate is already at four-twenty and the year's just started. This shit is crazy. What's wrong with these niggas out here? And they all young dudes. Listen to this, girl."

She started to read. "Chicago Fire Department, as well as CPD responded to a house on 59th and Bishop on reports of a fire. The house fire was eliminated by the Chicago Fire Department. Upon further investigation, the fire was ruled as a homicide after a black man was discovered in the home. The man, whose identity which has not yet been confirmed, seems to have suffered from what police believe to be a gunshot wound to the head from a large caliber weapon. Chicago Police would like anybody with information on this horrific crime, to please notify the Chicago Police."

"That's crazy as hell," Shakira replied. It was times like these, she was kind of glad YaYo wasn't out on the street. Chicago was at an evil time as the murder rate was steady rising. So many young black men roamed the streets of the Chi, with only one thing on their young minds, catching bodies.

Most of these young men were raised in single parent homes without their father. Or any authority figure for that matter, so they took to the cold streets of Chi-Raq to find acceptance and love from the gangsters in their neighborhoods. Chi-Raq was a jungle and the only way to survive the blood and turmoil was to be the predator, thus turning so many black youth into savages.

Shakira then started to think about her brother-in-law, Quavon. She knew what he was involved in as his name was ringing all over the city. She just hoped and prayed he would bow out the game gracefully before it was too late and he ended up like his brother YaYo, confined to a United States penitentiary or worse, buried six feet deep in the Burr Oaks Cemetery like her own brother, TJ.

CHAPTER 9

Suge stood in a full-length mirror checking his appearance. He was on his way to a new club that had just opened in South Memphis called Pure Passion. It was a new strip club owned by the nineties rap group called MJG. Suge had manifested to become one of the largest drug suppliers in Tennessee. He had only been in Memphis for five years as ice was coming from Compton, California.

Suge had managed to have major influence and dominance as he was a high-ranking Piru Blood gang member and accomplished planting his Los Angeles gang culture in Memphis, turning a lot of street cats in North and South Memphis into Bloods. As Suge preached the gospel of Blood politics, he was also able to flood the streets with cocaine and heroin, putting him on top of the drug game.

Suge looked at his appearance through his twenty-five-hundred-dollar Louis Vuitton shades. He was dressed to impress. This was an opening event, so he made sure he was flamed up, representing his allegiance to the Blood gang. The blood red Giuseppe suit jacket fit snug on his five-eleven athletic frame as his black Tom Ford jeans fitted him to perfection. To complete his outfit, blood red high-top Gioseppo shoes laced his feet. A 24K gold rope worth twenty-five grand draped around his neck, while the gold Audemar Piguet flooded with diamonds surrounded his wrist.

"Baby, you know you that nigga, don't you?" Kels said, walking up and hugging him from the back as he stood in front of the mirror. The smell of his Versace cologne almost made her come. Kels was Shug's side chick. She had been fucking with him since Suge had come to Memphis. She was wifey, until Suge had to serve a year in Mason Penitentiary on a gun charge. She had given one of Suge's workers some pussy, she ended up pregnant. Even though she chose to abort the pregnancy, Suge had found out about her disloyalty and hoeish acts through Facebook gossip and stopped fucking with Kels, and had the worker shot to death for the disrespect. Kels begged Suge to take her back, but he no longer trusted her. So, he used her for what she was worth, dropping off and picking up drugs. Her reward for handling those duties was nothing more than getting every hole in her body filled to capacity with Suge's meat, which she was sprung on.

Turning around, he faced Kels, who had on nothing but a red thong, swallowed by a fat ass that would put Nicki Minaj to shame. Kels was thick in all the right places. Wide hips, luscious lips and a snapback on the pussy was one of the reason Suge kept Kels around. Her peanut butter complexion and the naturally long, curly black hair fell to her back, gave her an exotic look. She was a bad bitch in the physical, but in the mental, she was fucked up.

"You already know I'm that nigga. That's why you fuck with me, cuz I'ma boss," Suge retorted, cocky as hell. Kels shook her head in the negative.

"Nope nigga, this why I fuck with you." Kels squeezed Suge's dick through his thousand-dollar jeans. It immediately began to swell just from her touch. She started to undo his designer belt buckle and he tried to stop her, but Kels wasn't having none of that. Before he knew it, his pants was down to his ankles and Kels was on her knees, freeing his nine-inch dick from the barrier of his Prada boxer briefs. Suge's cock throbbed as Kels held it in her hands as if it was a precious jewel.

She was always willing and ready to devour his meat. When sucking Suge's dick, she would try to suck the soul from him. She stared at his pole for a minute, admiring its length and width, before she took as much of him in her mouth as she could. The taste of his pre-cum coated her tongue as she began to suck hard on the mushroom head as she jagged on him. Suge could do nothing but let her pleasure him. He looked at his fine diamond flooded timepiece and the time read 11:15. He wanted to make it to the club by 12:00 so he could make his grand entrance, and fucking around with Kels was going to make him late. So, he decided to speed things up.

Suge laid back on the bed as Kels made his way over. Grabbing a fist full of her hair, he pushed her head on his dick, making her gag. Kels took care of her business while Suge fingered her asshole. He loved putting his finger in her tight brown hole as he knew it would bring him to the climax quicker. Suge had his middle finger in her tight spot as she tried her hardest to take in all of him. Two minutes later, Suge splashed her esophagus with warm gooey cum, which like the pro she was, she managed to swallow all of the semen. She continued to suck and grope Suge's dick and balls. He literally had to pry her off his tool.

An hour later, Suge pulled his Bentley Flying Spur into Club Passion. It was 12:15 and the club was jam packed, yet the line to get inside the establishment was wrapped around the corner. Suge pulled up to the front of the club and got out the red foreign whip. The valet parking assistant retrieved the keys from Suge.

"Take care of the Blood," he said, giving him the keys. The valet assistant got in the whip to go park it.

Walking inside the dimly lit club, all eyes were on the drug boss that just entered. A sexy redbone walked up with a sparkling bottle of Ace of Spades. She was short, about five foot three, with a small waist and ass that looks like it belonged on the back of a horse.

"Excuse me, sir, this bottle was sent to you from those gentlemen over at the table," she said with a seductive, flirtatious smile. Suge accepted the sparking bottle. Looking over at the table he saw it was his mans, 8Ball and MJG, who had the city of Memphis on lock. Their tape, *Comin' Out Hard* had made the group millions and they had been on and popping ever since. Suge raised his three-hundred-dollar bottle of Ace of Spades in the air, acknowledging his people, then made his way to the bar.

The atmosphere in the club was lit, weed smoke hung in the air like fog as YFN Lucci blasted through the speaker. Ballers popped bottles, as some of the baddest strippers in the south shook their money makers, in attempts to get some of the dead presidents that were being thrown around freely from hustlas draped in jewels and the latest designers.

"Let me get a double shot of that 1738, baby girl," Suge said to the bartender who looked like Kiesha Cole.

"Coming right up, honey," she replied as Suge pulled out a ridiculous wad of big faces.

"That's the boy right there. Ain't it, shawty?" Rockett asked after downing his shot of Crown Royal.

"Who, fam?" Choppa scanned the massive crowds of niggas in the club.

"The nigga with all that ice. With all that red shit on," Rockett replied. Choppa continued to search until his eyes rested on Suge, who was paying for his liquor and then started making his way to the VIP.

Choppa and Rockett had been in the club looking and waiting for Suge to come to the club. It was the luck of the draw. They didn't know if he was coming. They just figured by a new club opening up in South Memphis, the man that had control of Memphis streets would definitely make an appearance, and their hood instincts were right as they now had a vision of the "King of Memphis."

It had been two days since they killed Breed and Roscoe in the Berry Homes Projects. Their orders from Quavon was to give the drug dealers an alternative. Either hustle for G.B.C. or be laid to the pavement as Quavon wanted complete dictatorship over Memphis. Rockett and Choppa were subordinate to Quavon and the laws and policies of G.B.C., so the work they put in was out of love for the gang.

"So, how did we go play this game, fam?" Choppa asked.

"We go up there and holla at ol' boy and give him a proposition he can't refuse. Feel me, shawty? All you gotta do is follow my lead. This nigga a hustla, so he think with a hustla's frame of mind. If he about his money, he should be with it huge. Remember, it's best to have him in compliance. Quavon needs somebody down here to push the work. It would be easier to have a nigga like this character," Rockett said, standing up, grabbing his bottle.

"Breed and Rosco was hustlas. But them niggas bucked the style," Choppa retorted.

"Breed and Roscoe was workers. Suge is a boss. Two different entity's, shawty," Rockett replied, making his way to the VIP with Choppa in tow.

Suge was in the VIP, sitting on a couch, with about six exotic looking strippers entertaining him. He was having a good time, as the weed and alcohol ran through his blood stream. When Rockett and Choppa walked up his hand now rested on his 9 mm. Suge hardly moved with personal security, but would move relentless with the steel. Noticing the men approaching, he tapped the thick stripper that was sitting on his lap on her butt, signaling for her to get up, which she obliged.

"Can I help you two gentlemen?" Suge took a pull from the weed. Rockett offered the bottle of 1800 Tequila to Suge.

"Naw, I'm good, Blood. Just state your business," Suge calmly said, blowing out a thick cloud of smoke.

"I wanted to holla at you about some business. Anywhere we can speak a lil more private without muthafuckers all in the mix?" Rockett asked, looking at the strippers who were standing there, nosy as hell.

"Y'all ladies give me a minute, but this won't take long so don't go too far." The strippers walked away to go entertain another one of the many ballers in the club.

"Speak on it, Blood. I'm trying to have a good time and y'all niggas in the way." Rockett took the slight disrespect on the chin but kept his focus on the bigger picture. He took a seat next to Suge.

"Listen bruh, I'm a representative from the G.B.C."

What the fuck is the G.B.C.?" Suge questioned.

"We from Chicago, my nigga. We have a good thing goin and my superior sent us to get up with you and offer you a proposition."

"Is that right?"

"You see, we know you got Tennessee on lock and key and we just trying to network with good niggas that's getting to that bag."

"I'm listening," Suge said, lighting another blunt of Kush.

"It's like this, shawty. We are willing to drop you off bricks of the finest heroin once a month. The work is good and you can cut it to look like three different ways."

"What's the ticket on the bricks?"

"We charging sixty thousand a key," replied Choppa speaking up for the first time.

"Sixty thousand a key? The price a little bit high, Blood. My shit come from Cali and my shit can get cut eight times and still be a bomb, so I would be losing fucking with y'all niggas." Suge took another pull on the weed before he passed it to Rockett. The talk of money and dope seemed to put his defenses down. He could tell the men before him were hustlers by the jewelry that surrounded their necks and wrists. Suge could smell heavyweights by the aura that came from them.

"You probably think you got it sweet. But we know your shit is not consistent, you experience more droughts than a desert. You never feel a drought fucking with the G.B.C. We in with the cartel," Rockett said, throwing bait in the ocean, trying to catch a shark.

"What makes you think that? Where you get your info from, Blood, cuz you wrong as shit," Suge lied, He was getting a lot of weight from his Mexican plug, Hector, but a lot of times Hector would play games. Putting Suge on hold at times and he'd stop answering his phone, which would frustrate Suge.

"My nigga, we know more about you then you think."

"How is that?"

"Because the niggas you got hustling for you talk way too much, shawty," Rockett said, taking his Galaxy 6 phone off his Gucci belt. Scrolling through his phone, he pulled up some pictures and showed them to Suge. The pictures were of Breed, splattered face down in the parking lot with his brains leaking, and his sidekick Roscoe, shot to death inside the apartment. The shocked expression on Suge's face let Rockett know that Suge was oblivious to Breed and Roscoe's murders.

"You see, my nigga, cats like these is how niggas like us get football numbers in federal penitentiaries. We probably did you and more street niggas like you a big favor by downing these two goofies," Choppa said.

Suge sat back and soaked it all in. He knew nothing of the G.B.C. or the dude Quavon, but one thing for sure, he knew the representatives of the G.B.C. was head bussas. It was evident from the work they had just put in.

"So y'all saying you can front me the work on consignment? How many bricks will you be able to front?" Suge asked.

"How much can you move, Blood?" Suge thought about it for a minute. He wanted to see how heavy   G.B.C. was in the game.

"Fifty kilos," he blurted out. Rockett and Choppa looked at each other, before they both erupted in laughter. Suge felt slightly offended being at the butt of a joke.

Man... check it out, shawty," Rockett said, getting serious and back to business. "Fifty bricks of dope ain't shit to us. We was giving those two niggas twenty a month and they was faking with that. How about we start you off with a hundred of them. Let's just call it a trial run."

At the sound of a hundred kilos of soft, Suge's dick got hard. He had never touched that much work at one time, and if the two niggas in front of him wasn't the feds and on some real nigga shit, then he was about to elevate to another level of the game.

"Alright, Blood. That seems like an offer I can't refuse. But, I'm letting y'all know right now. You cross me, me and my Damu homies coming to the Chi to see all that shit, and we ain't gonna stop until that whole city is painted red."

"We understand."

"What's understood doesn't need to be explained, fam," Choppa replied standing up to shake Suge's hand. Rockett did the same.

"Now that we got all the business out the way, let's celebrate by fucking some of these fine ass bitches up in here. Everything on me," Suge said, making his way out the VIP to the stage to throw a few bands. The three men continued to smoke, drink and have a good time. Suge rolled out the red carpet, feeling he'd just secured the plug of a lifetime.

The club closed at 4:00 am. After swapping info, Rockett told Suge to be expecting them to contact him in the next few days. They had come to Memphis to take care of some Nation business and were now back on the highway headed back to Chicago.

"So, what do you think about ol' boy?" Choppa asked from the passenger seat of the Maserati truck.

"What I think about him doesn't mean shit, shawty. Once he receive the first shipment, then he tied in. This shit ain't no democracy, it's a dictatorship. The minute he acts like he's bucking, we busting his shit. Period." The G.B.C. was trying to reach new

heights of the game and the only way was to have complete dominance, not just in the streets of Chicago, but in the world.

CHAPTER 10

4 MONTHS LATER

It had been four months and seven days since YaYo had been taken to the SHU inside Pollock Penitentiary. He had been waiting for a disciplinary shot for an assault that he was involved in with the Alabama inmates in Unit C-1. since then, they had moved B.D. Pook and Harold on Range 3 with YaYo. They were two cells down from him. The time had been going by fast for YaYo in the SHU. His daily routine consisted of working out twice a day, reading and writing his manuscript.

YaYo had even heard from Mr. B. An inmate who worked inside the SHU on the sanitation crew had been given a kite or letter from Mr. B to give to YaYo, who was doing a set of crunches when the inmate discreetly slid the kite under the door. YaYo picked the taped-up letter off the floor that had his name written on it. After opening the kite, he saw the handwriting and knew it belonged to Mr. B. YaYo began to read.

"Yaton, I hope this special scribe reaches you in good spirits and peace, as it should. First and foremost, Allah is great and merciful and is the creator of life. Yaton, since we have met many moons, we have spoken on our creator, as well as our future and positive progress. I'm not going to waste the ink in this pen or waste your time preaching to you. I have gotten a chance to know you as a man, a brother and a child of Allah. I know your intentions are good and yet, I also know the environment in which we are confined to.

Every day is a test of our faith. Sometimes we are strong. Sometimes we are weak. We endure a lot. But always remember, Allah will never put a burden on your back which you cannot carry. I am not mad at you as I know you did what you had to do. Just learn from this. I have spoken to the captain in reference to you coming back to the compound. I was highly disappointed to hear you would be getting transferred to another facility, but appreciated it greatly to learn you would be designated to the S.M.U. program.

Yaton, I have been to the S.M.U. program twice. I believe the program will be beneficial to you. The solitude will give you time to focus on self. Evaluate self and mold self to be something great. You are in control of your own destiny, Yaton.

Now don't get me wrong. You will endure hard times and your faith will be tested on the regular. You are close to going home, YaYo and that's when the real test will begin. You have to learn what negative thinking errors are and find solutions and ways to combat them. The S.M.U. will help you more than it will hurt you. Work on yourself physically, mentally, and spiritually. Educate, meditate and elevate. It's all up to you, Yaton. I kept my end of the bargain, so trust and believe I expect you to keep yours. I will be looking forward to hearing from you soon. Insha Alllah. Take care, brother. With most respects, Mr. B"

After reading Mr. B's letter, YaYo had a different outlook on going to the S.M.U. program. He was going to use the program as a think tank to mold himself into the man he wanted to be, instead of the man others wanted him to be. He was at peak and he was going to face whatever came his way as a man and as a gangsta.

"Aye, YaYo!" B.D. Pook yelled out the door, trying to get YaYo's attention. YaYo got off the floor from doing his crunches and came to the corner of the door.

"What's good, fam?" YaYo yelled back. The range was always loud from inmates yelling out the door.

"Aye Scud, what you down there doing, B?"

"I was down here working out until you interrupted me."

"My nigga, you down there faking like shit. Aye G-Wayne, tell your celly to get off the door with that bullshit. His body look like a garbage bag that's full of water," B.D. Pook joked.

"Pook, you can't tell this nigga nothing, Blood. He think his shit up to par," G-Wayne yelled form his bunk. He was reading a book called *Blood of a Boss* by an author named AsKari. G-Wayne was supposed to have gotten out the special housing unit a few months ago, but had caught some more disciplinary shots for bucking in the recreation cage, holding it hostage. G-Wayne didn't care, to him doing time was doing time. Whether in the hole or on the compound.

"YaYo, send your line. I got something for you, Scud," B.D. Pook yelled down the tier. YaYo went to the corner of the cell door and grabbed his car. The tube would guide down the tier and whoever received it, would use their car to connect with the other. Thus, making it available for inmates to pass kites, contraband or whatever else could be transported.

YaYo grabbed his car and slung it under the door towards Pook's cell. The toothpaste tube glided down the tier as it stopped directly in front of B.D. Pook's cell. This procedure was called fishing and YaYo had it mastered. B.D. Pook slung his own car under the door. Once he had YaYo's car in his cell, he taped a small folded piece of paper to it.

"Pull fam," Pook yelled down to YaYo. YaYo pulled his string until his car was back in his cell.

"I got it, Pook," YaYo yelled back that he had the car back in his cell. YaYo took the tape off and unfolded it. Seeing the contents of the package, a smile came across his lips as he stared at the light green fluffy substance.

"Good looking, my nigga."

"Man, don't trip, fam. Just know the next one on you," Pook yelled back.

"Say no more, thug," was YaYo's reply. YaYo put the car back in the corner of the cell and tapped G-Wayne's bunk. "What's up, Blood?"

"Ain't shit. You trying to get high?" YaYo asked.

"What kind of question is that, my nigga?" G-Wayne asked, putting down the urban novel he was reading.

YaYo and G-Wayne were in the cell high as kites when two C.O.'s came to the cell door.

"Yaton Anderson, come to the door and cuff up," the CO said, opening up the food slot.

"What y'all want with me?"

"Today is the day of your S.M.U. hearing. Cuff up." YaYo did as he was told and stuck his hands through the food slot. After being cuffed, YaYo was led to a small room and sat in front of a television screen. On the screen was an older white man with gray hair. YaYo was having his S.M.U. hearing via television. The audio and video was set. The representative from the Bureau of Prisons began the hearing.

"Mr. Anderson, can you hear me?"

"Yes," YaYo responded.

"Very well. Mr. Anderson, for the record, can you please state your name and registration number?"

"Yaton Anderson, number 07505-424."

"Thank you. You are here for your scheduled hearing for your admission into the Special Management Unit at USP Lewisburg. Are you aware of that recommendation?"

"Yes."

"Okay, I will be reading you the disciplinary infraction in which you were formally charged with a 224 major assault on another person. Specifically, on September 9, 2018, inmates associated with the security threat groups, Black Gangster Disciples and Folks Nation, assaulted inmates from the geographical area of Alabama over a disrespect issue. You and others began assaulting inmates from Alabama upon observing one inmate strike another. Inmates associated with the Folks Nation then joined the assault.

You were observed on recorded surveillance, stabbing another inmate in a stabbing motion. The inmate suffered three critical puncture wounds. One to the kidney, one to the chest, and one to the inmate's lung, causing his lung to collapse from the blunt trauma.

It is the recommendation from the Federal Bureau of Prisons that you be admitted to a Special Management Unit for phase 1, 2, 3, and 4. Is there anything you want to say, Mr. Anderson, before a decision is made?"

YaYo remained silent. He already knew that no matter what he said, it couldn't change the outcome of his situation and that he was sure of.

"Alright Mr. Anderson. You will be admitted to the Special Management Unit of USP Lewisburg. If you choose to appeal this decision, just know that you have one week from today to do so. Good luck, Mr. Anderson."

The hearing lasted all but five minutes and just like that YaYo was designated to go to the infamous Lewisburg Penitentiary, where he would be housed with the worst of the worst that the Federal Bureau of Prisons had to offer. USP Pollock had no kiddie camp, but the S.M.U. program would truly be the ultimate test. It would test YaYo's mind, body and will. The S.M.U. was designed to break the hardest of men, as YaYo would soon find out.

YaYo laid back on his bunk, replaying his hearing. In a couple of weeks, he would be on a plane headed to Pennsylvania to USP Lewisburg. All he could do was remember the words from Mr. B...*Evaluate self and mold self to be something great.* YaYo made a vow to himself that he was going to focus getting his life together, he was going home in a few years. He was going to be on a mission to help these young black men and women find some kind of positive guidance to help combat the death and destruction that has plagued the city of Chicago.

If he wanted a fighting chance, he had to be equipped mentally and spiritually to do so. He was done with the prison politics, he couldn't go home to be a gang chief to his mother, to his brothers, to his daughter and baby mama. YaYo would die behind the walls of a federal USP as Yaton would be released from the belly of the beast.

CHAPTER 11

Two weeks later, YaYo's plane landed on a small air strip in Harrisburg, PA. This was his second time being on a plane since he had been in the feds. The first time was when he was flown from Oklahoma to Louisiana. He knew this was the way the feds transported their prisoners. YaYo was led off the plane shackled from hands to feet as he slowly made his way down the plane's steps. It was now the middle of winter and the wind chill in Harrisburg was below zero.

YaYo stood waiting with a slew of other inmates heading to different prisons on the East Coast. Several buses waited to be loaded with some of the B.O.P.'s heavyweights. YaYo read the signs on the front of the prison buses. USP Canaan, USP Allenwood, USP Hazelton and USP Lewisburg were just a few.

After standing in the bitter cold for fifteen minutes, YaYo was loaded on the bus headed to USP Lewisburg. Once on the bus, bag lunches were passed out to the prisoners, ten in all. YaYo sat in the back of the bus, trying his best to eat his cold bologna sandwich with cuffs on, which was close to impossible, yet he managed.

"How the fuck they expect us to eat tied to belly chains and shit?" Freddy said, trying his hardest to eat his lunch. Freddy was a Latin King gang member, who was also on his way to the S.M.U. for stabbing another inmate. He was being transferred from Big Sandy, a Location in Kentucky.

"Yeah, I know, they are wrong as hell for this," YaYo replied.

"Where are you coming from?" Freddy asked.

"USP Pollock."

"Oh, yeah? My big homie was down there. His name King Tino. He not there no more. The brothers got into it with some Louisiana cats and they transferred him to Victorville, California"

"Ya, I remember Tito, we was on the same unit. He the one taught me how to play chess. Where you from, my nigga?" YaYo asked, biting into his sandwich.

"I'm from St. Paul, Minnesota." The two convicts continued to conversate for the hour it took them to get to Lewisburg Penitentiary. Pulling up to the prison gates, the look of the prison was intimidating as it looked like an old castle. The red brick building was a hundred years old. Some of the coldest gangsters in the world had been sent to Lewisburg Penitentiary to serve hard time.

After being cleared at the gate by the guards in the guard station, the gates to hell opened and the prison bus was allowed to go though. Pulling in front of the prison, the bus stopped where about twelve guards standing post, waiting to lead the convicts into the concrete building that would serve as their home for the next eighteen months or longer, depending on their behavior.

"These crackers look racist as hell," Freddy said, noticing the big rednecks that wore blue coats with bold white letters that read USP Lewisburg. One of them stepped on the bus with a clipboard in his hands.

"Now listen up for your name. When I call you to the front of the bus, give me your name and number and get off the bus. Yaton Anderson..." YaYo stood and walked up the aisle of the bus as slowly as he could, as the tight shackles were cutting into his ankles. Once in front of the bus, YaYo gave the C.O. his name and registration number. "Yaton Anderson, 07505-424," the C.O. checked his name off on the clipboard and YaYo proceeded down the steps.

After all the inmates were off the bus, they were pat searched then led into the penitentiary. All of them were standing in a single file and one by one, they were called into a small room where there was a body scan machine.

"Step up to the machine. Keep your head facing forward and don't move" the C.O. said with authority. YaYo could tell by the damp smell inside the prison and the dirty walls that the prison was definitely old.

Twenty minutes later, the C.O.'s came to the holding cells with plastic bins. One of them stopped in front of YaYo's cage.

"Strip out, boy. Take all your clothes off and place them in the bin." After stripping, YaYo stood naked as the day he was born.

"Let me see your hands, palms up. Under your arms. Open your mouth, lift your sac. Turn around and spread your cheeks. Let me see the bottom of your feet." YaYo did as he was instructed. He hated the strip search part of being processed in, but at this point he had no control. He was the property of the federal government. After giving the guard his clothing sizes, the C.O. went to get his prison-issued uniform. YaYo dressed and was handcuffed and taken to see S.I.S. and the captain of the Lewisburg Penitentiary, this was protocol for all inmates.

When he was let into the office, nine guards all occupied the small office. The captain and the S.I.S. Lieutenant sat behind the large desk. The S.I.S. Lieutenant had a folder in front of him that contained YaYo's file. YaYo stood in front of the desk with handcuffs. The pale-faced lieutenant, who resembled Al Bundy from *Married With Children*, opened the folder.

"Yaton Anderson, transferred from USP Pollock. Gang affiliation G.B.C., status active. Projected release date, 2021. So, Mr. Gangbanga. Do you know why you was sent to Lewisburg?" the lieutenant asked, looking up from the folder.

"For a disciplinary infraction," YaYo replied, being short.

"For a disciplinary infraction, huh? Well, it says here you and some of your gangbanging buddies stabbed a couple dudes over disrespect issues. Is that true?" The lieutenant spit a wad of chewing tobacco into an empty Coke bottle, waiting for YaYo to respond, which he didn't.

"Look like we gotta killa on the compound, huh?" the captain intervened.

"You listen here, you maggot fuck. That gangbanging shit gets no fucking airplay down here. We despise you lowlife son of a bitches. If it was up to me, instead of wasting good taxpayers' money, I would just take you out back and put a bullet in your black ass head. You weak-spined cluster fuck." The C.O.'s laughed out loud like they were at a stand-up comedy show.

"Now, my advice to you is that you stay the fuck out the way. Because I tell you this, gangbanga, if your name come across my desk one fucking time, I'm going to make sure you remember my white face for the rest of your black life. Do I make myself clear?"

YaYo's blood was boiling at this point. The only thing he could envision was him putting the captain in a truck of a stolen vehicle at gunpoint, and then taking him somewhere to blow his brains out. YaYo felt his inner demon start to surface, but he remained calm. "And since this nigger seem to not know how to speak, make sure he is housed in D-Block. Welcome to USP Lewisburg, dip shit." The captain sneered before YaYo was led out and taken to his housing unit.

YaYo was taken to D-Block, also known throughout the prison as dog D-Block was for inmates with extensive behavior. Most inmates housed on D-Block were problematic inmates, who carried life sentences and was sure to die and be buried in a prison cemetery. They cared little about their lives or the lives of others, so they were quick to assault other inmates or staff, so the administration treated them cruelly. Their mail was tampered with, their recreation was limited as well as their showers. Depending on the mood of the officers, their meals might be brought up to their cells an hour later than the scheduled time it was supposed to be served.

YaYo was escorted down the long hallway of D-Block. Inmates came to their doors to look out the window to see who had arrived on the new. Today was Thursday, and Thursday was bus day, the day for new arrivals. The C.O. that was escorting YaYo stopped in front of a cell with the number 18 on it. Taking the key off his utility belt, he used it to unlock the padlock on the food slot. "Lawrence, cuff up," he commanded to the inmate on the other side of the door. YaYo could see the man was kind of tall so he had to bend down to stick his hands through the food slot.

Once the C.O. had the cold cuffs around his wrists, he spoke into his walkie talkie that was clipped on his shirt. "This D-Block. Pop cell 18... I repeat, pop cell 18."

A couple seconds later, the cell door slid open. YaYo now saw the man that stood behind the odor. He was six foot one, with a brown-skinned complexion and waves in his hair. The look on his face bore menace and intimidation. YaYo let a mug plaster on his face to match the man's aggressive demeanor, letting him know he was with the shit if need be.

"Anderson, step in," the C.O. commented. YaYo walked into the severely small cell and stopped right in front of the door. This was a security tactic as when the C.O. locked them in, he would be the first to get his cuffs off. He had heard stories of inmates crushing their celly while they still had handcuffs on. YaYo wasn't taking any chances. If his new cell mate was on bullshit, YaYo would at least have an equal opportunity to defend himself. "Close cell 18," the C.O. said, after YaYo stepped inside the cell.

Once the cell door closed, YaYo stooped down so the C.O. could get his cuffs off. After he did so, YaYo stood and moved out the way so the celly could get his cuffs off. With both inmates uncuffed, the C.O. closed the food shot and locked it. "Anderson, I will be back in thirty minutes with your bed roll." The officer walked off. YaYo turned to face his cellmate, who was rubbing his wrists from them being too tight.

"Where are you from, fam?" he asked.

"I'm from Chicago, Illinois," YaYo responded by leaning his back against the wall and folding his arms across his chest. On point.

"Oh yeah? I'm from Chicago myself, what spot did you just come from?"

"I just came from the USP Pollock."

"Pollock, huh! I was there about eight years ago. I just came from Florence, Colorado. The name's Nino." Nino stuck his hand out in greeting, which YaYo accepted. The two shook hands. Nino was glad that at least his new celly was from around his way, but he also knew that meant nothing in the S.M.U. A lot of dudes sent to the program were burnt out, no matter where they were from.

"Check it out, fam. I don't know what kind of time you are on, but the only way we can cell together is your paperwork straight. I know you just came in, so you ain't got your property yet, but it should be here by the end of the week at the latest. When it gets here, we gone exchange that work. I'm letting you know right now, if you are hot... snitch, then I'll let you get out of here peacefully.

But, if I got to find out I been sleeping with a rat for a week or so, then we gone wreck, my nigga. It is what it is."

Nino was given a life sentence for drugs and a snitch had given it to him and he would be damned if he shared a cell with an oversized rodent. A slight grin came over YaYo's lips. He was glad Nino was on paperwork because he was on the same time, but he was going to let Nino know in so many words that he was also 'bout that life.

"Check this out, my nigga. I was on lock for about four years and I told you I just came from USP Pollock. I was there for the whole four years I was down. You said you was there, so you already know every car on the compound checking that paperwork and if niggas ain't straight, they getting ate. I came in with a life sentence, but I put in a 2255 motion and my motion was granted and I got back in court. The cop that put the bogus evidence and statements on me routed them and they removed the life, but kept time charged with the gun.

And they made me out within a hundred and twenty months. I'm finishing that up now. I get all my paperwork in my property: sentencing transcript, docket sheets, 2255 motion and my trial hearing. I got transferred from Pollock because me and my niggas crashed out with some Alabama niggas and tha knife got pushed and shit got bloody. So, I'm letting you know right now, I'm a thousand percent nigga. And I'm like you, Scud. I hate rats."

Nino let what YaYo just spoke ponder in his thoughts. He could tell right then and there, he and YaYo would get along. He could see the thoroughbred in him, as the eyes were the key to the soul. Nino had been in the B.O.P. for almost twenty years and had been around a lot of different breeds of niggas from all over the United States.

The feds was where thugs came to vacation. Some for several years and some for the rest of their lives. Nino was one of the ones the federal government had sent to the feds where thugs came to vacation. His out date read, "deceased." Nino knew that a lot of street niggas that faced federal prosecutors folded. It was a saying that "half the niggas in the feds old and the other half wished they told," so he took precaution when dealing with niggas. But he knew that YaYo was different, as real recognize real.

"I feel you, YaYo, and I respect that. Make yourself at home. This gone be your spot for at least eighteen months."

"Yeah, I heard," YaYo said, putting his mattress on the top bunk. The two gangsters continued to chop it up for the rest of the night. Nino let YaYo know what was going on around the S.M.U., as well as the do's and don'ts.

YaYo knew it was going to be a long eighteen months. He couldn't wait to get his property so he could get comfortable. He also needed his address book and stamps. He wanted to write to his people. He had to let Shakira know he had finally made it to Lewisburg and he also wanted to write his daughter.

Thinking of Shakira, the picture of Jamari clouded his thoughts. He couldn't help but to think about how he would raise him if he turned out to be his son. It was now 10:30 pm and the lights in the cell went out, ending his first night in Lewisburg Penitentiary, the S.M.U. program. YaYo let his thoughts consume him as he drifted off into a deep sleep.

S. Allen

CHAPTER 12

Omega pushed the Dodge Hellcat down the Dan Ryan Expressway as KI, Ace and Goon trailed behind him. They were on their way to pick up Marcus from Cook County Jail. Marcus had gotten arrested the night before for drunk driving after crashing his SRT Durango truck on the west side, and now the T.H.C. was on their way to bond him out.

It had been four months since they robbed and killed Roy. The six kilos of heroin and the hundred and fifty geez of dope money had put them on. Not to mention, they were about to get another hundred racks for the truck. It was easy for them to get the dope off. It was all profit, so the six keys was dumped off at fifty thousand a brick, netting the team three hundred grand.

T.H.C. was all the way up, but the destruction they were about to cause in Chicago had just begun. They were almost at a half mil, but that was nothing, they wanted to be millionaires and they were itching and willing to kill anybody to achieve their dreams.

Omega switched lanes in the Hellcat as he looked at the time on his Frank Muller timepiece that was sprayed with ice. The watch alone had cost a hundred thousand by itself. Seeing it was 11:45, he knew it was a chance they would get caught up in the midday traffic and if they didn't post Marcus's bond by 12:30, he wouldn't be able to bond out until 3 pm. Marcus would be pissed, but it was what it was.

As Omega glided the whip through traffic, he began to reflect on his life. Only four months ago, he was sitting in a trap spot with a razor blade, baggies and a scale, bagging up a few ounces of crack. He would pull all-nighters in severe winter conditions, ducking the law as well as his enemies, just for a measly few thousand dollars. He had been in the streets his whole life. And now he was at the top and steady climbing the pyramid.

Omega was born Ramon Mitchell on the operating table in Cook County Hospital, twenty-eight years ago. His mother Helen had birthed him as a teenager, with a life in which she had no direction. Omega's father at the time was forced with the responsibility of being a father, which he chose to elude and abandoned his son and his son's mother.

By the time Omega was four years old, his mother wasn't able to provide for her only son. Doing what she thought was right, she gave him up to the state, the Department of Children & Family Services, or DFCS. Now a state baby, Omega was adopted by a white married couple in Napierville, Illinois. With Omega being their only child, they spoiled him to the core, until he was ten years old. That's when Omega's problematic behavior began. His anger issues started to emerge, as well as his rebellious attitude towards his parents.

Omega would lash out at them when he didn't get what he wanted. By the time he was thirteen years old, his violent temper was something his foster parents couldn't deal with, so they put him in treatment. Even after the costly therapy, Omega remained violent and full of rage, so with nothing else to do, his parents gave the rights to their child back to the state of Illinois and left the responsibility of raising young Omega back in the laps of DCFS.

Living his life in and out of group homes, Omega was intrigued by the thug life, the lure of the streets and what was confined in them was enough to make Omega dive head-first into a life of crime. At first it started with smoking, drinking and hanging out, trying to be accepted by his peers on the south side of Chicago, and quickly elevated to guns, drugs, and murder. Catching his first body had transitioned him from a petty criminal into an armed career criminal, as spilling blood seemed to be the only thing to quench his thirst for violence, thus molding him into a killa.

It wasn't until he met Ace, who was a hustler, that he learned the game in dealing drugs. Ace taught Omega how to cook and bag cocaine and that, added to his arsenal, qualified Omega as a thorough street nigga on the come up. He experienced everything that came with the streets. The ups and down, the good the bad, as well as the love he had for Ace.

That love was bonded by trials and tribulations, and blood. The two goons had made a vow that one day they would be rich and get up out the hood. That pact was made when they were kids and now as grown men, it was time to get out of the contemplation stage of life, as they were now in the action stage of achieving their dreams.

Forty minutes later, Omega pulled up in front of the Cook County Jail on 26th and California. KI pulled up and parked behind him and got out of the driver's seat of the Cadillac Escalade. She was dressed conservatively in a sundress with flower prints, the Jimmy Choo heels laced up around her toned calves. Her freshly done dreads were tied into a neat ponytail as Cartier frames covered her eyes, giving her a sophisticated look. Ace remained sitting on the passenger seat smokin a blunt of Kush, going through his Instagram.

"I'll be right back," she said, closing the driver's side door. Walking up to Omega's Dodge Hellcat, Omega rolled the window down as she approached.

"What's good, you got all the info you need?" he asked KI as she walked up and stuck her head in the whip, her Dolce Gabbana perfume greeting him. Omega admired her exotic beauty, while each movement of her cleavage and MAC lip gloss had him wanting to taste her flavor. When KI walked towards the steps of the court-house, her ass cheeks bounced inside her sundress like two Wilson basketballs. Omega groped his dick through his jeans as he wanted lustfully. He had known KI forever and not once had he attempted to fuck her. Her tomboyish demeanor always threw him off, but lately, she had been showing more of her womanly side. Omega started to envision hitting KI from the back with a bed full of dead presidents laid beneath them. To say he was starting to feel something for KI would be an understatement. She was fine, thick, and throughout the City of Chicago she was known as a certified shooter, as her murderous reputation installed fear in some of the hardest niggas in the city.

Omega's erotic daydream was broken up when his phone beeped as it sat in the cup holder. Grabbing it, he saw that it was Ace trying to video chat him. He accepted. Ace's picture shown on the screen with smoke as he exhaled Kush smoke through his nostrils.

"What's good, nigga? You trying to hit this?" Ace asked, holding the blunt up for Omega to see.

"Hell naw. And why are you smoking in front of the jail? You hot as hell, causing all that undue heat," Omega schooled. He knew Ace was young, black, and reckless and his head was concrete. He thought he knew everything, so you couldn't tell him shit. That was just Ace.

"How am I hot and I'm behind the tint? Man, fuck these police," Ace retorted.

"That's your problem. It always fuck this, fuck that. Niggas better get on point."

"Yeah, I get it," Ace replied, dismissing Omega's minor lecture. "But check this out, thug. I was just on Facebook and they saying the nigga Blue Cheese supposed to be coming to the city to perform. He supposed to do a show at the United Center. So, you already know what I'm on. What you think?" Ace asked, hitting the Backwood. Omega looked at the crazed lunatic on the screen.

"You holler at KI about it?"

"Not yet. I just stumbled upon this. You know I fuck with the nigga CK-30. He supposed to be opening up for the nigga, so he just put me on, feel me?"

"You talking about CK-30 with the cocaine-white Wraith? Fuck with the cards and shit?"

"Yeah, that's my mans." Omega let the robbery lick ponder in his mind. He remembered seeing Blue Cheese on YouTube and the nigga definitely had on plenty ice. He had a cool mil around his neck, not to mention, his wrists had something chunky on it as well.

"Holler at KI and Marcus see what they say. As for me, I'm all in," Omega said.

"Say no more," Ace replied and ended the video call excited about the lick he was about to put together for his squad. He needed this to go smooth, so he needed it to be an inside job. Letting the wheels turn on his tank, he came up with the perfect plan. He took a strong pull from the blunt and tossed the blunt duck out the window and placed a phone call to his mans, CK-30.

An hour later, after being processed out of Cook County Jail, Marcus walked out the front door as a free man after KI posted his ten-thousand-dollar-bond. The long restless night he spent laying on a cold bench inside a holding cell had him tense. But what really had him perplexed was the two detectives that came to speak with him. Crashing the Durango truck and drunk driving were the least of his worries. After searching the vehicle in which Marcus was the sole occupant, police recovered a Glock .19 handgun with a thirty-round extended magazine. Marcus sat in a small interrogation room when the two black detectives walked in.

"What's good, playa? I'm Detective Jones, this here is my partner, Detective Flowers." Detective Jones was about five foot eleven, with an athletic build, brown-skinned with long French braids. He wore black cargo pants, black Nike ACG boots and strapped over his neck was his badge, letting his duties to serve and protect be visual. Detective Flowers was a little on the heavy side, five foot eleven and two hundred and fifty pounds of brute, clean shaven and black as night. He was a no-nonsense type of guy and was quick to use violent tactics. Detectives Jones and Flowers had been partners for five years as Homicide Detectives.

"What y'all want with me?" Marcus asked, scared as hell. Detective Jones had the Glock .19 inside of an evidence bag. He placed it on table in front of a handcuffed Marcus.

"Have you ever seen this weapon before? I mean, you had to have seen it. It was found in your vehicle." Marcus remained silent.

"You want to do this the hard way, huh? Well, check this out, fuck nigga, this gun has your fingerprints on it. And how about this? That gun was used in a homicide about four months ago. A man was shot and killed on 59th and Bishop. You know anything about that?" Detective Flowers said, lighting a Newport cigarette before passing it to Marcus, who accepted it with his cuffed hand. Marcus took a strong pull from the cancer stick as sweat ran down the side of his face. Detective Jones noticed and went in for the kill.

"Now, we already have the story. We know you were the shooter. We also know you didn't act alone. Now, you can either help us help you, or you can answer for this single-handedly. Which means you get stuck with the body. The choice is simply up to you."

"Listen, boy. You got some serious shit with you. We already hip to you and who you are running around with. My advice to you is to look out for yourself, because I'm quite sure if the shoe were on the other foot, your friends would definitely throw you under the bus. We can indict you with just having the murder weapon. You having this pistol in your possession connects you to the body, and there isn't a jury in the United States of America that wouldn't find you guilty. So, if you want to roll the dice with your life, then go right ahead." Detective Jones pulled out his contact information from the pocket of his vest and placed it in front of Marcus.

"Now, we are going to let you post bond. But don't try no funny shit and try to get ghost, because we got a close watch on you. Remember what we said, try to save yourself because one of y'all is going to take the hit for that boy's body. Who takes the hit is completely up to you."

The interrogation played over and over in Marcus head all night. How could he be so stupid to get caught with a gun? A gun he used to shoot and kill another individual at that. There was no way he could let T.H.C. know that he got caught with it. The same gun they had instructed him to get rid of. The same gun he told them was at the bottom of Lake Michigan. They had killed people for less, and his blatant security breach would be the cause of his ruin.

Being on federal parole, Marcus knew he had to get out of Cook County Jail as soon as possible, before his parole officer was notified and he was placed on a parole hold. So, when he heard his name come over the loudspeaker in the holding cell being told to pack up, he was geeked to know he would have another chance at freedom. For how long, he was definitely unsure of.

Walking out the glass doors of the courthouse building with KI, the bright sun hit him in the face, causing him to squint his eyes as exhaust fumes and the smell of near restaurants mixed together with the smell of the Chicago streets and his freedom. Marcus noticed Omega's Dodge Hellcat and KI's Escalade truck parked at the curb. Omega beeped the horn and waved him to the whip.

"What's up, Killa? A nigga hungry as shit, I'm a hop in with this nigga and tell him to stop and get something to eat," Marcus told KI.

"We right behind y'all," was her only reply before she made her way to the Cadillac truck. Marcus hopped in the passenger seat of the Hellcat.

"What's good, Joe? You look like shit," Omega said, shaking up with Marcus, whose braids were looking a lil ruff from tossing and turning on his folded-up shirt all night.

"Yeah, I know right. Good looking on bonding a nigga out. Straight up."

"Man, you already know we family, ain't none of ours gone be stuck sitting in no county jail if we can help it, and if a nigga do, we gone make sure you live like a fucking king," Omega said genuinely. He loved his people and would die and kill for his gang.

Marcus saw the sincerity in Omega's eyes and felt the loyalty in his words. He wanted nothing more than to tell Omega about his run-in with the two homicide detectives, but he didn't know how the crew would take it. He figured he would just go day by day. *Maybe the detectives were pump faking and they were just fishing for information,* he thought. If they had him red-handed, then he would have been charged for the murder and would've never left out the county jail. Hopefully, for his sake, his thoughts were correct.

Omega pulled off into the hustle and bustle of the Chicago streets. Pulling a blunt of sour diesel Kush from the ashtray, he put it to his lips and sparked it. Taking a strong pull, he inhaled the smoke before passing it to Marcus.

"I'm glad you out of there, my nigga... I need to holler at you," Omega said, blowing out smoke.

"What's good?" Marcus retorted, hitting the blunt.

"Like I was telling Ace, y'all niggas got to be more on point. All that driving drunk, crashing whips and shit, that's causing you unnecessary heat. Y'all already know what we are out here doing and y'all acting like we ain't on no felony shit. Always remember, it's when niggas get hot, that's when niggas get popped."

Marcus hit the weed again before passing it back to Omega. Omega glanced in the rear-view mirror and saw the Escalade behind him. He could see Ace bouncing in his seat throwing up H-C with his fingers, apparently geeked up off some rap music. Omega just smiled and shook his head at the young demon.

"Aye, but check this out, Scud. I was hollering at Lil Ace and he was telling me about the nigga Blue Cheese coming to the United Center to perform."

"Oh, yeah? What that got to do with anything?" Marcus asked, his eyes low from the love they were smoking.

"We gone try and bring them niggas a move. Him and his camp that come with him. I know one thing, all the ice they be wearing, when that hammer is in their face, they better take it off slow or I'mma let it blow. Man, these niggas goofy for real. Take their shit and make them buy it back from us." Omega sneered, ready to eat.

"How do we go about it tho?" Marcus asked.

"Don't even trip, we 're gonna let Ace handle that part of the stain. When he says move, that's when we move. See if we can get a few mil off this ugly lil nigga."

T.H.C. was at the Home Run Inn Pizza Parlor on the city's west side, eating and politicking about the Blue Cheese demonstration. Everybody seemed to be on the same page pertaining to the lick, everybody except Marcus, whose only thought was of him getting caught with that gun. And now he was about to put himself in another situation, that would nine times out of ten end with homicide. All he could do was just play his position, and at the same time, find a way out of the game before it was too late.

CHAPTER 13

"Damn girl, you feel so good," Quavon moaned in ecstasy while he gripped Bella's wide soft hips. Sade's "No Ordinary Love" played softly in the background as the smell of love hung in the air like fog. Quavon had flown Bella in from Florida. He had been so busy conducting his business in the streets that he had neglected the attention of Bella's body and sexual needs. So, he'd flown her first-class and they were now at the Sybaris Hotel suite, getting it in.

Bella gripped her two firm 38-DD breasts in her manicured hands, at the same time toying with her nipples. Her hair was a mess and sweaty from the workout she was enduring, bouncing up and down on her man's hard cock. Quavon stared in the eyes of his beautiful woman as he matched her, thrust for thrust. Her exotic looks made him want to shoot his load inside her, but his stamina was on point from the Grey Goose and the Percocet he had consumed. Leaning up to the soft titties, he took one of her nipples in his mouth, at the same time spreading her sweaty ass cheeks, digging deeper into her love box.

"Quavon, oh my God, baby, I feel you in my stomach. Quavon, you so deep, papi."

Bella purred softly, licking him on his neck. He loved when she talked dirty to him, which heightened his lustful primal rage. Turning on her stomach, Bella tooted her phat ass in the air giving Quavon VIP access to do as he pleased. Quavon stared at Bella's pussy lips that looked like two gorilla knuckles stuck together, from the back. Pussy juice coated the insides. Quavon knew he had a bad bitch. She was his Beyoncé and he was Hov. Grabbing her by the hips, he stuck the tip of his dick in her love canal. Teasing her.

"Baby, stop playing with me and beat this up."

"Shut up. I got this," Quavon replied, before he thrusted his throbbing meat inside of her as fast as he could. Bella almost lost her breath from the width of him, as he pulled out nice and slow before he went back. For ten minutes, he long- and slow-stroked her at a steady pace, bringing her to two powerful orgasms, coating his dick with her vanilla cream. But he was far from done. Quavon slid out of her pussy and spread her cheeks, exposing her tight brown forbidden hole.

He started by planting wet sloppy kisses on her cheeks, then running his tongue down her crack, and tonguing her asshole. Bella went crazy and reached back, grabbing his waved head, applying pressure for him to put his tongue deep into her booty, she immediately began to cum again.

After giving his woman the ass eating of her life, Quavon spit in the palm of his right hand and lubed himself with it and in one swift motion, he was balls' deep inside of Bella's ass. Her highness and the warmness of being in her ass was too much to bear. So after about fifteen strokes, he exploded inside her in three strong spurts.

"Ahh shit, baby girl," he said, pulling his semi-erect penis out of Bella's ass.

Quavon collapsed on his back, his body sweaty from the work he had just put in on Bella's body. Bella got up to go to the bathroom to clean herself up, while Quavon grabbed the half-smoked blunt of loud out the marble ashtray and lit it. He took a strong pull and filled his lungs with smoke as Bella was coming out the bathroom with a warm soapy hand towel. Quavon watched her intently as she crawled her flawless body in the bed, took his now soft love muscle in her hands and with care, cleaned him up. After wiping him down, she curled up next to her king, accepting the blunt from him taking a pull.

She exhaled before she said, "Baby, I was talking with Robert a couple days ago."

"About what?" Quavon probed, taking the blunt back from her.

"He was telling me about this Irish guy from Boston."

"And?"

"The guy's name is supposed to be Frank. And he deals in diamonds."

"Bank Roll Buddy ain't mention nothing. And what this got to do with me?"

"I was just thinking, baby. This drug and thug shit is a lil played out. Don't get me wrong. You handle your business, but I just feel you are worth so much more, and you can accomplish more than what you are. For real, baby, you can really be on some boss shit," Bella said, squeezing Quavon's dick again, which was now swelling in her hands from her touch.

"So, he was telling you about this cat, Frank, who deals in diamonds. So now what? It had to be more dialog in the conversation then that," Quavon stated.

"I was thinking you could make a power play with this dude. Invest and progress, baby."

"How much you think I should invest?" Quavon asked her, only knowing one thing about diamonds and that was they brought plenty of money. He was already all the way up. He had about four mil in street cash and another one point two million in the field. He had Chicago, Indiana, Missouri, Detroit and Memphis on lock and was raking in plenty of dough.

Bella got serious as cancer. "I was thinking three point five, just to get your feet wet. The turnover on your money should net you no less than ten million," Bella answered, jacking Quavon's now rock-hard dick at the same time.

Quavon laid his head back on the pillow. Ten million dollars would put him all the way up. He had been getting money for the past four years. He had cars, clothes, houses and the G.B.C. was flooding the streets with bricks of heroin and cocaine he received like clockwork from his cartel plug. He had the streets of Chi-Raq in his clutches as his shooters kept his position in the game concrete.

Doing business with this Frank character would definitely be up for discussion, so he was going to call a meeting with his G.B.C. chain of command Crusha, Reggie-G, Choppa and Rockett to get their opinions. So, a sit-down at the round table would be a must, then he would go and politick with Bank Roll Buddy to get more information on this nigga Frank and then he would proceed.

Quavon's thoughts were broken when he felt the warmth of Bella's mouth on his pole. She stared up at him with her brown eyes, giving him head. Quavon put his hands in her long curly hair, forcing her head to go further down on him, causing her to gag. But quickly, she got back in control of the task at hand.

An hour later, after another fuck session Quavon slid from under Bella, who was deep asleep from the good dick she had just gotten. After showering, Quaon got dressed. He was about to rotate in the battlefield, so he was dressed for the job. He rocked a pair of fitted Armani jeans, a tight black Polo V-neck T-shirt, and a crispy pair of patent leather Space Jam Jordan's adorned his feet. A thirty-two-inch white gold Cuban link chain wrapped around his neck, letting YaYo's G.B.C. charm sprayed in ice hang to the center of his chest.

Tucking his compact .357 Glock in the small of his back, Quavon grabbed his iPhone and his keys off the island and left. He had paid for the room for two weeks, so Bella was straight. She would be upset when she woke up to find him gone, but she would get over it. He had more important things to do than lay up. He had some Nation business to attend to.

Quavon pulled up to a row house project complex on 137th and Low on the city's south side in the hunnids. Pulling into the apartment complex, he noticed his team was in attendance as he saw Crash's Range Rover truck, Rockett's Maserati truck, Choppa's AMG and Reggie-G's S-Class Benz. Quavon activated the stash spot inside his whip to get the ounce of strawberry Kush he had just copped from a weed spot on Chicago Avenue and Ridgeway. He knew his men had greedy lungs, so he was going to supply the smoke.

Walking in the trap-spot that was used to discreetly hold G.B.C. meetings, Quavon was greeted with the smell of high-grade marijuana. The chain of command sat at a glass table. Their attention was focused on the dominoes game they were involved in. Seeing they had already started their smoke session, Quavon tossed the ounce bag of loud on the table.

"Man, shawty come in here throwing that huff-ass weed on the table. Like that shit some gas," Rockett said, slamming his domino down.

"Nigga, whatever it is, I bet your ass smoke it. Thirsty ass nigga!" Quavon joked.

"Let 'em know something, Quavon. Niggas always complaining but ain't never putting nothing in the blunt," Reggie-G intervened, standing up to give his lil potna same dap and a thug embrace.

"What's good, bro? How are you?"

"You already know, Crusha. Trying to stay low. Only thing we can do now is maintain," Crusha retorted. Quavon took a seat at the table. Taking the .357 from the small of his back, he laid it gently on the table. He grabbed the ounce of weed, dumped its contents out and proceeded to break the weed down and roll blunts.

"Aye Quavon, have you heard from the big homie YaYo lately?" Choppa spoke while he wrote down his score after scoring on Rockett. Quavon licked the blunt to seal it.

"Yeah, my momma got a letter from him early this week. You know they transferred fam from the spot he was at. They sent him to Lewisburg, Pennyslvania to some shit called the S.M.U. program. He has to be there for at least eighteen months. He said it's a 23-1 lockdown," Quavon informed as he lit the tip of the blunt.

"What the fuck he do for them to send him there?" Choppa asked.

"I guess him and some homies got into it with some other niggas and some niggas got stabbed up. Davon said he talked to him before he got shipped but I guess at the program, you can only use the phone once a month or some shit!" Quavon passed the blunt to Choppa.

"That shit crazy. Bruh in that bitch cutting the fuck up. You already know he protecting this G.B.C. brand." Choppa admired YaYo's gangsta. To him, YaYo was the hardest nigga to come up outta Chicago. He had followed in his footsteps and put in plenty work for the gang chief and to him, YaYo was that nigga. Choppa took a pull off the blunt and at the same time, reached in the pocket of his Nike joggers, pulling out a large wad of money. Without counting a single dollar, he tossed the thick wad on the table.

"Send that to YaYo for me. Tell 'em it's from Baby Choppa."

"Oh, it's from Baby Choppa, huh? That's so sweet," Quavon joked, picking up the money, thumbing through the hundreds and fifties. Feeling outdone, Rockett did the same, tossing a large wad of cash on the table, as did Reggie-G and Crusha. In total, the money came up to twenty-three geez. Quavon cleared his throat.

"This the business, my niggas, as y'all know we moving through the bricks at an alarming rate. Castilino even dropped the price on the work, because now we move it so fast. But the times is changing, my niggas we gotta start moving with the time. Yeah, we standing on niggas with the work, but that's pebbles compared to rocks. I think it's time to raise the stakes." Crusha rubbed his goatee.

"Speak on it, youngsta. We are listening."

"What would y'all say if I told y'all I had a strong connect for diamonds?" Everybody looked at each other with a state of confusion on their faces.

"So, you say you want to get in the game of selling diamonds, sounds a lil risky to me, my nigga," Reggie-G spoke up.

"My nigga, everything we do is a risk. We in the game. In a game you can either win or lose, our aim is to win. But fam, we all gambling without either win or lose, our aim is to win, but we all gambling with our lives. I'm trying to take us from thousandaires to millionaires, you feel me?"

Crusha thought about what Quavon was kicking. He was from the old school and he knew the value of pure diamonds, and if Quavon could get his hands on the right quality, then they were sure to get to some millions.

"So, who we dealing with and what's the ticket?"

"That's a good question, Crusha. I'm a get up with Bank Roll Buddy and get all the facts to this shit, just give me a couple days," Quavon replied. He had got put on by Bella, but he had to holler at Bank Roll Buddy to get more in depth.

"So, are we all on the same page, or do some of y'all feel different?" Quavon asked his squad.

Rockett took a pull of weed. "I'm all in, shawty. You know I'm on whatever y'all on."

"Count me in, nigga!" Choppa applied ready for whatever.

"Quavon. You haven't steered us wrong yet, youngest and I trust your judgement with your family." Crusha knew Quavon's potential and his leadership was strong as he was a replica of his incarcerated friend, YaYo.

"Reggie-G, what's good, fam? What are you thinking?" Quavon asked. He noted Reggie-G was in deep thought. Reggie-G looked Quavon in his eyes. He trusted Quavon, but something just didn't sit right, they were getting plenty of money moving the work, and now here was Quavon popping up, talking about some diamonds. It wasn't that Reggie-G didn't trust Quavon. He simply just didn't trust Bank Roll Buddy, point-blank period! But not wanting to not give Quavon his support, he obliged to the new hustle.

"Alright, Quavon, I'm with it. But I'm letting you know right now, youngsta. If your lil cracker friend happens to pull some bullshit, trust and believe his ass gone make the 9:00 news," Reggie-G vowed, giving Quavon a thug embrace.

"What's understood, Reggie, don't need to be explained, my nigga," Quavon replied.

"Now, since that's out the way, my niggas, what the bizness with our boy Suge out in Memphis?" Quavon asked, splitting another blunt in half.

"Shawty all good. He is still grabbing the same ten bricks, but he is consistent with his paper," Rockett retorted.

"Good, that's what I like to hear. Listen, put another ten kilos on his shipment and send him a plane ticket to Chicago. Tell fam I want to get up with him. We gone show the boy Suge how bosses kick it. Maybe it makes him want to step his hustle up."

"Say no more, fam. I'm on top of it," Choppa said, being subordinate to the authority.

The G.B.C.'s chain of command continued to get high and discuss Nation bizness. There were countless opportunities to take advantage of. And the G.B.C. was trying to capitalize off all of them. Since being in the streets, Quavon had elevated and it had all come from moving with the jewels YaYo had instilled in him years ago. Quavon grabbed the rubber-headed stack of cash and put it in an Aldi's grocer bag.

"I don't know what y'all about to do, but I got some runnin around to do, y'all already know. G.B.C. and be safe!" Quavon stood, giving all his men a pound before leaving the spot.

Now that he had the support of his squad, he could proceed and get up with Bank Roll Buddy to get more detail on the diamond hustle. His palms were itching at the thought of the millions he was about to stash in his ceiling, the money was about to flow like the Nile River. But first, he had to stop at the nearest Western Union, to flood his brother's commissary account with G's!

CHAPTER 14

Back Inside Lewisburg Penitentiary

It was 5:45 in the morning and YaYo was up making his bed. In another twenty minutes, the C.O. was going to walk down the tier to sign inmates up for showers and recreation. All inmates wanting a shower or recreation would have to be up, beds made and cell in compliance. Failure to do that would get the inmates banged, crossed out on showers and recreation.

Every morning, YaYo and Nino would get up twenty to thirty minutes early, just to be on point. YaYo had been at USP Lewisburg for two weeks now. He learned that he wouldn't be able to use the phone until he was there thirty days. He had sent mail to his mother Karen and his baby mama Shakira, letting them know he was safe and at Lewisburg. Now he was just waiting for them to respond.

YaYo knew that being at the S.M.U. would be a test and he would have to practice extreme humility and patience, if he wanted to have a chance at completing the program. YaYo was told by his counselor at Lewisburg that he would be given book work in parenting, anger management, responsible thinking. The assignments would have to be completed in order for him to pass to the next phase at the program.

There were four phases in the S.M.U. The primary goal for the S.M.U. was to take the most violent, malicious federal inmates, isolate them from the rest of the general population and at the same time, give them assignments that would help them combat their extensive criminal thinking errors. Most of the men serving time at Lewisburg were goons with no conscience, and their respect was measured on how much violence they unleashed, or how much money they got off the yard selling drugs.

YaYo's days were structured to the core. Breakfast was served through a slot at 5:00 am. Showers were on at 7:00 am Monday, Wednesday, and Friday. Recreation was done at 12:00 in the afternoon. At this time, YaYo and Nino would be escorted to the recreation cage, where they would be able to exercise for about an hour or less, depending what kind of mood the C.O. was in. It could be less than the mandatory hour they were supposed to get.

After recreation, YaYo was led back to his living quarters, where he would spend the rest of his day working out, reading, writing in his manuscripts and building with Nino. YaYo stood looking around the cell to make sure nothing was out of place. Hendricks was a racist C.O. who prided himself on coming to work making inmates' lives a living hell, instead of doing his eight-hour shirt and going the fuck home. He would ban you from showers and recreation for a wrinkle in your blanket. He was surely an asshole.

"Cell 16. Recreation and shower sign up," Hendricks said, standing outside with a clipboard in his hands.

"Two for recreation, two for showers," YaYo said, holding up two fingers like a peace sign.

"Move out the way, boy," C.O. Hendricks said in his Nazi voice. He hated blacks. YaYo moved to the side, he knew how to play Hendricks, he just paid him no mind. Hendricks scanned around the cell with a mean mug on his face, looking for something out of place. He found none, so he wrote YaYo and Nino's names down on the clipboard, signing them up for both shower and recreation before he moved to the next cell.

Thirty minutes later, two C.O.'s came back to the cell and opened the food slot. YaYo turned his back to the door and squatted down, sticking his hands through the food slot. The C.O. secured YaYo's hands in a pair of handcuffs, and then placed a black metal box over the chain of the handcuffs. It was called the black box and it was used to prevent inmates from slipping out of the handcuffs. After his hands was secured behind his back, YaYo stood up and moved to the side to allow Nino to get his cuffs on. Once both inmates were cuffed, the C.O. radioed control to pop cell 16.

YaYo and Nino were led out of the cell and to two small shower cages. They were uncuffed and allowed to take a five-minute shower, which was timed. Returning from the cold shower, YaYo got dressed. He was making a cup of lukewarm coffee when Hendricks came back to the door.

"Aye Lawrence, you know somebody on the first floor named 6-10?"

"Yeah, them my people. Why, what's up?" Nino probed.

"Well, it's seems he got into it with his celly last night. So, we have to move him on the third floor. Is it cool if he recs with y'all, or is it going to be a problem?"

"I told you, one of mine, put him in the cage with us."

"Alright, Lawrence, I don't want to shit out of you two," Officer Hendrick threatened before he walked off.

"Who is 6-10, celly?" YaYo asked out of curiosity.

"He... 6-10 is one of the GD's. He been in the system about twenty. He a lil burnout, but he a good nigga. Even though he GD, he on Muslim time. I guess he got into it with his celly last night. Matter fact, hold up real quick." Nino stood on the toilet so he could reach the vent.

"Aye yo, New York!" Nino yelled in the vent.

New York came to the vent. "Nino, what's up, B?" New York yelled back into the vent.

"Aye, my nigga, what happened with 6-10 and his celly last night?"

"Aye, you hear me, B?"

"Yeah!"

"Yo son, shit was mad crazy. My nigga... 6-10 punished the old man while he was making salat."

"He put the knife in him?" Nino probed.

"That's a fact, son," New York replied. Nino shook his head. He knew 6-10 was throwed off and the situation probably could have been avoided. Something that was minor had quickly turned major.

"Alright, good looking. On another note, who you got on the game tonight?"

"What kind of question is that? The Knicks, son."

"That's what I like to hear. Bet thirty stamps since you like them so much. You love them, die with them."

"Who are you talking to like that, B? Run that shit!"

"Bet," Nino replied, securing his gamble for the night. Even in the S.M.U. gambling was big.

"Damn, that shit crazy. This nigga stabbed his celly while he was making salat," Nino said, stepping down from the toilet. Nino had been in a couple spots with 6-10 and each time, 6-10 blew the yard with some knife play. This was his fifth time in the S.M.U. Nino was close with 6-10, because not only was he a GD, but they were both from Chicago Heights. Beyond 6-10's reckless, violent behavior, he was loyal to Nino and his loyalty ran deep.

An hour later, YaYo and Nino were in the recreation cage doing burpees, when they saw the C.O. escorting 6-10 toward their cage. Showing all of his thirty-two teeth, 6-10 smiled hard. The C.O. opened the cage and 6-10 entered. After getting his cuffs off his wrist, 6-10 walked up and embraced Nino.

"What's up, big homie?" 6-10 greeted.

"That's what I'm trying to figure out. What's good with you?" Nino asked him, pertaining to the situation with him and his celly. As 6-10 looked over at YaYo as if he was pondering if he could speak freely around him, Nino noticed it.

"He's official, fam. You already know if he's in the cell with me, he a thousand." YaYo hadn't gotten his property yet or his paperwork, but Nino had been around and was a certain convict. He had the third-shift C.O. look him up on the computer and check his credentials. He came back A-1. But Nino also told YaYo he still had to see the original paperwork. YaYo wasn't tripping, so 6-10 proceeded to tell Nino about the demonstration he had just laid down.

"Man… Ock, they was all the way bogus. You know it's a sissy on our range. So, this nigga waits till I go to the shower, I should've known he was on some bullshit when he didn't want to sign up for shower. But anyway, he sent the punk a letter. I heard him holler out the door to the boy and ask him did he get it. I asked him about it when I got back from the shower. Ock straight lied to my face."

"So, you asked him about him hollering out the door about sending the boy a letter?" Nino asked, trying to see if 6-10 made his move with facts or objectivity. Reacting without facts is what 6-10 was known to do.

"The whole tier saw that nigga fish the letter to that sissy. He put it on Allah. So, I crushed him," 6-10 defended, feeling no remorse for his actions. Nino just shook his head.

"Check it out, 6-10, this my celly YaYo. He for the city too. YaYo, this my mans, 6-10," Nino introduced them.

"What's good, fam?" YaYo greeted, shaking 6-10's hand. The three convicts continued to conversate until they came to cuff them and take them back to their cell. The administration had moved 6-10 to the third floor and range with YaYo and Nino. He was now only three cells down, in cell 19. While being escorted back to the building, the C.O. informed YaYo that he had to go to R-D to get his property, it had finally arrived from the USP Pollock. YaYo was taken to get his property. Some of his property was not allowed at USP Lewisburg, so it had to be sent home, donated or destroyed. YaYo was allowed twenty-five pictures, two sweat suits, one radio, one pair of headphones, twenty-five letters and his legal papers.

YaYo made sure he grabbed the manuscript he was working on called *Drill Season*. Everything else YaYo told the C.O. they could destroy. YaYo liked to travel light anyway.

YaYo was back in the cell putting his property away, while Nino was in his bunk reading his Holy Quran. "Man, they made me get rid of a lot of shit," YaYo complained, passing Nino a yellow manilla envelope containing his paperwork. Nino put down the Quran and accepted it from YaYo.

YaYo started to look through the twenty-five pictures he was allowed to have. HIs eyes rested on a picture of Jamari. Ms. Sanchez had sent him some pics of his supposed to be son. The little boy had the same features as his daughter Shamira. YaYo still hadn't talked to Shakira about Jamari. He knew it would destroy his family, but at the same time he wouldn't deny Jamari a father, as he knew what it was to not grow up without one. It wasn't Jamari's fault that he was conceived and brought into this cold world. YaYo would not let Jamari go through that.

His own biological father was killed in a car crash when he was only three years old. He was sent to Chicago as an innocent child, but the streets had parented him into a savage street scholar, imbedding in him the rules of survival and finesse. But there were times when he had yearned for the love of his real father. Looking at the innocent child in the pictures, YaYo silently vowed that if Jamari was truly his seed, he would want for nothing, and he would raise him to be smart, independent, ambitious and goal driven so he would grow up to be a boss.

It was a week later when YaYo was allowed to use the phone for a fifteen-minute phone call. He could only use the phone once a month, so he had to either call his mother Karen, or his baby mama. The decision wasn't easy, but he needed to hear from his mother. He figured he would call Shakira and his daughter next month, but he needed to find out how his mother was and the situation with her moving to Orlando with Darrell. YaYo waited before the C.O. did a round. The C.O. did a walk-through on the range every fifteen minutes.

"Aye C.O. cell 16," YaYo yelled out the cell door, trying to get the cop's attention. "Who next on the phone? I'm trying to make a call."

"When I make my next round, I will pass the phone. Until then, stop yelling out my door," the C.O. said with authority before he walked off down the tier, continuing to make his rounds. Twenty minutes later, YaYo was laying on his bunk when the C.O. opened the slot and passed him the phone.

"Good looking, C.O." YaYo grabbed the phone from off the food slot.

"I'll be back in fifteen minutes," the C.O. said and closed the food slot. YaYo pulled the phone cord inside the cell. YaYo dialed his mother's number. She answered on the fifth ring.

"You have a collect call from Yaton, from a federal correctional facility. To accept this call, press five. To refuse this call, hang up. To block this number, press seven." Karen pressed five with the quickness. "This cell is subject to monitoring..."

"Hello, son, how are you?"

"I'm good, Ma. How have you been doing?"

"I'm doing good, son. I got your mail, I was going to write you back, but I have been having your daughter over here. Shakira been picking up a lot of hours at the shop lately," Karen informed him.

"Listen, Ma. I only got fifteen minutes and I can only call once a month."

"Baby, what kind of place they got you into and you can only call me once a month?"

"Ma, it's a long story, but what's going on with you and are you still moving to Florida with Darrell?" The phone went silent for a minute. "Ma, you still there?"

"Yaton, me and Darrell have chosen to try and make it work, and I think moving to Florida with a fresh start would be a good idea."

"What about the shop, Ma? You know I got that for you."

"I was thinking maybe you could let Shakira run the shop. She is great for the job. She is conducive to the business."

"What about Davon, Ma? He went to Chicago?" YaYo asked about the wellbeing of his brother. He didn't have to ask about Quavon, as he already knew he was ten toes down in the city, doing him.

"Davon has his job, so he's going to stay in Chicago, plus you know he is not going to leave Quavon. He will be a fine son."

"What about Grandma Honey? Who's going to take care of the lil lady?" YaYo questioned.

"Son, Granny is not going to leave the city. She will be okay, and plus Shakira and Shamira. You know Granny is not going to leave Shamira, that is her pride and joy. She will be fine, son," Karen assured. YaYo really didn't like the fact that his mother was moving all the way to Florida with Darrell, or the fact that Darrell had just appeared back in his mother's life after so long, and she was making the choice to move to Orlando with him. Away from her immediate family.

But YaYo loved his mother to the point as long as she was happy, he would support their decision. YaYo would leave the ball in Darrell's court. If he ever admits he chose to ever cause discomfort in his mother's life, then killing Darrell would be a part of his parole plan. He would punish Darrell for the old and new.

"You have one-minute remaining," the recorder said on the phone, letting them know the call was about to be terminated.

"Ma, this phone is about to hang up. I hope you are making the right choice, just know that I'm supporting you. I will talk to Shakira about the shop, and tell Granny I will be contacting her soon and send everybody my love and respect."

"Okay, son, I will. And don't forget to pray, Yaton," Karen said as the call was terminated, leaving the dial tone in both of their ears.

"Phone up!" YaYo yelled out the door to inform the C.O. that he was done using the phone and could pass it to somebody else.

"Everything all good at the crib?" Nino asked YaYo, going over YaYo paperwork.

"Yeah, everything's all well, fam. My ma about to move to Florida with her busta ass husband. I just hope she makes the right decision," YaYo replied. Nino could recognize the worry on YaYo's face.

"One thing about it, YaYo. You are in federal prison, my nigga. This is temporarily your world, so you have to focus on you and your surroundings. Leave everything else in the hands of Allah, feel me?"

"Yeah, I feel you, bro. I just can't wait till this hit is over with, so I can continue my life." YaYo climbed back on the top bunk. The S.M.U. wasn't bad, once he thought about it. One thing it did do for him was give him a lot of solitude and time to think. He had a lot of changes to make in his life and he was going to use this time to do it.

Karen had just hung up from talking to her son. She knew that he would feel some kind of way about her moving to Florida with Darrell. But the fact of the matter was that she loved her husband. In the past, she knew Darrell didn't treat Yaton like he did Quavon and Davon. For that reason alone, she let him start a life without him. Sending her son to Chicago was one of the hardest decisions she had to make, now she was feeling she had made the wrong decision. The streets of Chi-Raq had turned her precious firstborn into a killer and drug dealer.

Endless nights, she prayed to God to forgive her for sending her son to the murder capital of the world, only to become a statistic to a life of crime. Karen told herself she was going to accept her punishment from the good Lord, when they came. As of now, all she could do is pray for her family and their health and safety. Even though Darrell had been gone, he now wanted to come back into her life. No more was he the jealous insecure husband he used to be. She could tell he'd made a drastic change in his life.

He was humble, genuine and caring. Darrell was also on his way to being a corporate giant, his company was starting to do numbers and that he was grateful for. Darrell going to see YaYo in federal prison showed that he was remorseful about how he treated YaYo as a child. Karen wasn't going to condemn him for his past, who was she to judge anybody?

So, she forgave him, her heart and mind was strong and her subconscious mind was telling her she was making the right choice. She prayed about it and just put it in God's hands that everything would be all right, for everybody that she loved.

CHAPTER 15

Ace sat on the passenger side of the cocaine-white Wraith as CK-30 slid the expensive whip down Lake Shore Drive. Ace had gotten up with CK-30 about some serious business, robbing a platinum-selling recording artist from Miami, Florida named Blue Cheese.

"Is his bank as big as he be making it seem?" CK-30 asked.

"That's exactly what I'm trying to say, my nigga. Them niggas be having in millions of dollars' worth of jewelry around their necks. I'm trying to take a look at that shit, and plus, we have to send a message to niggas."

"What's that?"

"That this Chi-Raq and when niggas come to the city, they gotta holler at The Homicide Crew, cuz we need our cut. Cut us in or cut it out!" Ace vowed. CK-30 laughed out loud.

"What, nigga? You think this shit a game? Niggas ain't playing about this shit."

"Nah, I ain't laughing at you, my nigga, I'm laughing because y'all niggas is crazy as hell," CK-30 said, accepting the blunt back from Ace. CK-30 was a product of Chicago's south side, on 69th and Indiana, from a hood called Kuwait City. The neighborhood was a war zone, and at the time was the reason for a lot of bodies popping up on the south side.

The two had known each other since elementary school. Even though they were a part of two different gangs, with Ace being groomed as a Gangster Disciple and CK-30 being a part of the Black P Stone Nation, the two of them were compatible and formed a solid friendship.

CK-30 had transitioned from a petty heroin dealer to swiping bogus credit cards. This hustle later in life had put him on top and his bag was all the way up. CK-30 dressed in only designer clothes and drove nothing but foreign whips. With a slew of Instagram followers and Facebook friends, CK-30 used his street money to finance his position in the rap game and was known to open up for rappers doing concerts in Chicago. His parties were always lit, thus bringing out the city. "So, how are we gonna do it? A nigga ain't trying to go to prison fucking with y'all wild ass niggas," CK-30 said, hitting the blunt of sour diesel Kush.

"You already got the keys to the city, Moe, all you gotta do is get up with the nigga manager. Tell 'em you wanna open up for him. Come on, fam, you act like you don't know how this shit go."

"What's my cut? Make it worth my time, Ace."

"Don't even trip, 30. You already know I'm gonna look out for you proper," Ace retorted.

CK-30 thought about it as he let it ponder. He was a hustler to the bone and he already knew how rappers always flossed their best jewelry, especially when they did shows out of town. Plus, if the robbery went right, nobody would know he had anything to do with the crime. It was a win-win situation for him.

"Alright then, Ace, but this shit has to be executed righteously."

"Don't even trip, my nigga. This is how it's gone play out, fam." CK-30 pulled up and parked his Wraith on 69th and he, Indiana, and Ace smoked blunt after blunt while they politicked on the robbery of Blue Cheese. Shit was definitely about to get real in the city.

YaYo and Nino were in the recreation cage, waiting for the C.O. to bring 6-10 in the cage, so they could perform their daily workout that consisted of five hundred burpees, five hundred Navy Seal push-ups and five hundred crawl-outs.

"Man, it's hot as hell out here," YaYo said, taking off his shirt. It was ninety-five degrees in Lewisburg, Pennsylvania. The heat was scorching.

"What's taking the police so long to bring 6-10 down here?" Nino asked as he stretched his legs. The C.O. had to escort and each man from the cells to the recreation cage. Ten minutes later, two correctional officers escorted 6-10 down the walkway toward rec cage number seven's cell.

"I'm not assigned to his cage, I'm in cage number seven," Nino heard 6-10 say to the cop.

"You either go in there or go back to your cell. You don't dictate shit here at Lewisburg, boy!" the C.O. responded, opening the cage for 6-10 to enter. Not wanting to go back to his hot cell, 6-10 obliged and stepped inside the cage with the Muslims. Once the cage was locked, 6-10 stuck his hands though the slot so the C.O. could take his cuffs off. After uncuffing the inmate, the C.O. smirked at 6-10, then walked off to do a fifteen-minute round.

As 6-10 looked around the small rec cage, it was occupied by two more Muslim inmates in the corner, involved in what looked to be a serious conversation, so 6-10 paid them no mind.

"Aye 6-10, what's good, fam? Why they put you in that cage?" Nino yelled from two cages down.

"Man, I don't know, folks. They on some bullshit," 6-10 yelled back, stretching his arms, about to do some pull-ups from off the top of the rec cage, which was equivalent to a pull-up bar. YaYo watched the two Muslims intensively. They seemed shady. The one with long dreads began to tie his dreads in a ponytail as 6-10 was on his second set of pull-ups.

"Aye Nino, your mans cool in the cage with them two niggas?" YaYo asked. Nino looked over at the cage more closely to the men's demeanor and noticed the shady facial expressions on the two Muslims.

"Aye 6-10, stay on point, Ock," Nino yelled, while 6-10 was in the middle of his set. The two Muslims waited until the C.O. walked off the walkway, before they made their move. The baldheaded Muslim with his face completely tattooed, grabbed 6-10 by his legs in an attempt to pull 6-10 off the cage. Since 6-10 now knew he was being attacked, he held on for dear life with all the strength he could muster.

The other Muslim with dreads pulled a plastic shank from his ass checks and started to stab 6-10 in the stomach and chest. Feeling the knife puncture and pop his skin was the worst feeling he'd felt in his forty-five years of life, but yet he held on, knowing if he fell, they would possibly murder him in the recreation cage.

Nino watched helplessly as his friend was punished in retaliation for what he had done to their Muslim brother. The Muslim with the dreads, whose name was Kadafi, climbed up the rec cage and was now face-to-face.

"You shed our brother's blood, so your blood will be shed." He sneered before he started to repeatedly stab 6-10 in the face, puncturing his eye, jaw and head.

Soon, 6-10 had no more strength as he fell to the concrete. The Muslim who was holding 6-10 by the legs was now on top of 6-10, pinning his arms to the side, while Kadafi continued to give 6-10 that wet-work, stabbing him until the C.O. saw the assault on the camera that sat in the corner of the recreation cage.

They stormed the cage in riot gear and pepper spray guns. Upon seeing the C.O.'s, the Muslims stopped the violent assault, retreated to the back of the cage and laid flat on their stomachs, complying with the correction officers. Laying in a puddle of his own blood, 6-10 was flat on his back. After the C.O.'s got the two assailants from the cage, 6-10's body was loaded on a stretcher and airlifted to the nearest hospital.

Later on that night, YaYo was in the cell. Today had been a violent day in Lewisburg Penitentiary, 6-10 had gotten stabbed up in the recreation cage and another inmate housed in B-Block was stabbed by his D.C. cellmate as he slept. USP Lewisburg was deadly, as it was evident from the day's events.

"Aye Nino, YaYo!" New York yelled in the vent downstairs. Nino got out his bunk and went to the vent.

"What's good?" Nino yelled back.

"Aye yo, they say your man ain't make it, B. He went all the way out."

"How do you know, fam?" Nino asked, not believing what he had just heard.

"The lieutenant just left off the range and informed us that the incident in the rec cage was now a murder. It's a fact, son," New York replied.

"Alright fam, appreciate it," Nino said with a heavy heart. He had just lost a friend as well as a brother and it hurt him to the core. Nino climbed off the toilet and got in his bunk and pulled the sheet over his head.

YaYo had heard New York word for word. Not to mention, he had witnessed the work the Muslims had put in before his very own eyes. He knew by the way 6-10's eyes looked as they placed him on the stretcher, that it was over for him. He took in 6-10's eyes as if the Reaper was choosing his soul.

YaYo had seen death a few times throughout his life and knew 6-10's life was over. YaYo wanted to give his celly some support but figured he would just give him some time.

The next morning, YaYo was awakened by the food slot being opened. It was 5:45 in the morning and breakfast was being served. YaYo hopped off the bunk to grab the two trays for him and Nino. After grabbing the two trays, he set them at a small table in the cell.

"Aye, Nino. You signing up for rec, fam?"

"Nah, I'm good," Nino said from under the blanket. He wasn't ready to get up and face the day, still in his feelings about 6-10's murder.

"Well, I'm not going out either." YaYo grabbed his notebook and pen and climbed back on the top bunk. Last night, he was captivated by his son Jamari's picture. He stared at it for hours. He knew Jamari was his son without a doubt as he held the same features as YaYo's daughter, Shamira. It was crazy that he had brought a child into the world from behind the walls of a federal penitentiary when he was serving a life sentence. Now knowing that he would touch the streets again, he wanted to be a part of Jamari's life as he had always wanted a son to bear his name. He was grateful that Jamari was born. YaYo sat down to write Ms. Sanchez.

"Damn, ma. You dropped a hell of a bombshell on a nigga, but I'm glad you was a woman about it. I respect you for that, shorty. It's crazy how things happen in life, my grandmother used to always tell me God put people in your life for a reason, and he takes people out of your life for a reason. You already know about the change in my situation. That shows God is real.

I know you can respect the fact that I want a DNA test on Jamari, even though in my heart I feel he is mine. I just want to make sure. Shorty, I don't know what's going to become of us. Hopefully, a beautiful relationship. Honest and trusting.

You know I have a wifey and a daughter, and to keep it a thousand, I haven't even told her about you and Jamari, but I know the time will come when I have to. Like I said, I just want to make sure. Just know that if I am the father, I'm going to man up and take care of my responsibilities. That's my word as my word is my bond. I will keep in touch. Much respect, YaYo."

YaYo folded the letter, stuck it in an envelope and put the P.O. Box address on it that Ms. Sanchez had given him. After putting the envelope under his mattress, he laid on his bunk, thinking about Ms. Sanchez and the lustful fifteen minutes he had with her at USP Pollock. He was sure in that fifteen minutes, Jamari was conceived. YaYo's thoughts were of his family, his freedom and making it out the gloomy Lewisburg Penitentiary. He vowed nothing would stop him from going home. YaYo made a silent prayer and drifted back to sleep.

CHAPTER 16

Quavon and the G.B.C. pulled into the parking lot of the United Center on the city's west side. The last time he was here, his twin brother Davon had gotten shot by TB and his cronies. That incident did not go unpunished as TB had lost his life for it. Quavon sat behind the wheel of his new Rolls Royce Cullinan. He'd dropped three hundred and fifty thousand on the exclusive SUV. Bella occupied the passenger seat. This was a major event, so it was a must he sported her beauty on his arm.

Choppa sat in the backseat, he was Quavon's personal security for the night. Quavon was his boss, so the two Glocks would be used to protect the safety and well-being of the leader for the G.B.C. Following behind Quavon was Reggie-G and Crusha in the Benz wagon, with Rockett and Suge in the Jeep Cherokee SRT. Quavon had flown Suge from Memphis to Chicago to show him a good time and plus, he wanted to speak with him face-to-face about time serious business.
Suge had a lot of influence in Memphis and Quavon knew that shit was worth much more than what Suge presented, and Quavon wanted to flood him with more bricks then the ten he was sending him monthly. He was trying to get his numbers all the way up.

"Damn, this muthafucka gone be lit," Choppa said from the backseat, while he rolled up a few blunts of Kush to sneak inside the United Center. It was hard finding a spot to park as the parking lot was flooded with foreign vehicles every major or minor drug dealer, hustla, and bad bitch in the city was there to see Blue Cheese.

"I know it's at least a hundred million dollars' worth of niggas in this bitch," Ace said excitedly from the passenger seat of the Cadillac Escalade truck as he watched a nigga getting out of a Rolls Royce truck.

"Hell yeah, it's an armed robber's heaven out here tonight," Goon stated from the back seat. Omega was behind the wheel. KI and Marcus tailed behind them in the Dodge Demon. The Homicide Crew was cruising the parking lot, trying to find somewhere to part.

Tonight, they were about to lay down a crucial demonstration. They were about to jack a known rap artist.

Inside the exclusive Sky Box in the United Center, Quavon watched the concert, accompanying him was his girl Bella and his G.B.C. family. The atmosphere was lit as four-hundred-dollar sparkling bottles were clutched in the hands of young men and women who represented the Chicago hustle.

Quavon looked over the massive crowd of the Chicago underworld. He was dressed in a Ralph Lauren Purple Label blazer that had cost him a few racks, as his fitted, smoked gray Michael Kors jeans with red stitching that matched the blazer. On his feet was patent leather Jordan's. His jewelry was wet, while both his earlobes held two blue diamonds, the pinky ring on his finger held enough ice to freeze Africa. That represented his Don status in the streets. It was the same ring he took off Top Cat the night he shot him in the head.

Bella stood next to him, taking small sips of the bottle of Nuvo. She wasn't big on drinking, but tonight was a special occasion, so she was sipping a little something. She definitely looked like the wife of a drug dealer in her Vera Wang. The outfit looked like it was painted on her stallion frame. Lugano princess cut diamonds froze her ears, while a Martin Katz chain hung around her neck. Bella looked like she should have been at a ballroom dance floor, rather than a rap concert.

A bottle of Rémy XO rested in one hand and a blunt of sour diesel Kush in the other. A Parmigiani Fleurier flooded in diamonds surrounded his wrist. Quavon was out tonight to make a statement to the streets, that he was the dictator of the streets of Chi-Raq and that the G.B.C. would forever be a force to be reckoned with.

"This is nice, Quavon, I just think that it's a little over dressed for the urban stuff," Bella said sarcastically. Quavon paid her subliminal word play no mind.

"You cool, baby. We just out having a good time," Quavon said, pertaining to Suge, who was enjoying himself.

"Yeah, I know. I just think you can do something more earning with your time, don't you think?" Quavon took a strong pull from the blunt before he responded.

"What you mean by that?" he asked, blowing smoke through his nostrils.

"What I mean is you keep wasting your time with this midget shit when you can be a giant." Quavon turned to face her with a sneer plastered across his lips.

"What the fuck you just say?" His tone was menacing.

"All I'm saying, Quavon, is I'm trying to put you on some major money and you are straight bullshit. You still haven't even hollered at Robert yet, have you?"

"How do you know I haven't hollered at Robert?" Quavon asked with a raised eyebrow,

"Because I know you haven't. You need to get your priorities straight, Quavon," Bella said before she stormed out of the Sky Box. Quavon wanted to go after her but thought against it. Tonight wasn't the night to argue with Bella, he had not come to the United Center to fight with his girl. He came to make his presence felt and to holler at Suge about some serious business. He would deal with Bella later.

"Aye Suge, check it out, big homie," Quavon yelled over to Suge, who was being entertained by a couple of Chicago's finest chicks.

"Naw, you the big homie, Blood," Suge said, walking up to Quavon, who was standing on the balcony of the Sky Box. Quavon passed the blunt to Suge.

"How are you enjoying my city?" Suge hit the weed.

"I ain't gone lie, my nigga, on Blood. Y'all got this shit on smash. Straight up, Blood."

"You know... Suge, it wasn't all me, fam, I'm just holding down what my big brother left before he got sent to the feds. But that's another story. I flew you out here because I wanted to holler at you face-to-face. You know niggas ain't talking over no phones at this level of the game."

"I'm listening," Suge said, passing Quavon back the blunt.

"You have been doing well with us as far as moving the work, but let's keep it real, Suge. I know you can move more than ten bricks a month. Am I right?" Suge nodded his head confirming that Quavon was correct. "Listen, my nigga. Do you think you can move a hundred kilos a month?"

Suge's eyes got big as saucers after hearing a hundred kilos. He knew the Quavon and the G.B.C. was some heavyweights in the game and it was no doubt they were about their business when it came to that murder game. Suge had done his homework on Quavon and his reputation and it had come back valid, but being in his presence, he knew Quavon was a boss from the way he articulated his words, how he moved, as well as the way he dressed.

"Hell yeah, I can move a hundred of them things a month," Suge retorted. Truthfully, he had Memphis on lock and key, and also had his hands in Nashville, Tennessee, where he had a lot of Blood influence there. Quavon and the G.B.C. knew that Suge was ready to elevate, he just hadn't brought it to Choppa and Rockett yet.

"Okay then, that's what it is. Say less, my nigga. When you receive your next shipment, be expecting a hunnid. And always remember, fam, communication is everything. We can always try and fix mistakes, but violations will not go unpunished, are we understood?" Quavon said, giving Suge eye contact as he spoke, letting him know that this conversation would not be repeated ever again.

"Don't even trip, Blood. Let's get this paper," was Suge's only reply as he shook Quavon's hand.

"Let's get to it though. Now since we got that out the way, let's enjoy this show, it looks like shit lit down there." Quavon nodded towards the stage where CK-30 had the crowd going crazy as he performed his new track titled, "Had To Drop My Op."

"Let's get closer to the stage. I wanna take some flicks." Quavon, Suge, Rockett, Crusha and Reggie-G made their way out the Sky Box.

Pussy nigga, I be dropping 40 got the dumb out on it
Did a track with Durk and I went down on it
Draco, Draco got a laser. Red dot.
Got locked up for a body. Cue I had to drop my op.

The crowd was going crazy as CK-30's violent lyrics graced the airwaves inside the United Center. The stadium was packed shoulder to shoulder, and everybody was turning up! Ace walked through the crowd, throwing up his gang and representing The Homicide Crew. The liquor and ecstasy flowing through his bloodstream, combined with knowing what he was about to do, had him geeked and feeling like the murderer he was. He was ready to put some work in.

"Man, this bitch lit. It's so many hoes up here, look at shorty over there," Ace said, nodding in the direction where an exotic looking chick was standing off to the side by herself. Goon turned to see who had his homie's attention.

"On chief. Shorty like that, look like that and got a few dollars too," Goon said.

"Well, I'll let you know when I come back," Ace said, walking off towards the direction of the Latin beauty, he was on her heels.

"Ace wild as shit. But I love that nigga," Omega said, hitting the blunt of loud before passing it to Goon.

"Check your boy out," Goon jokes.

"Excuse me, Ms. Lady," Ace said, getting Bella's attention.

"Yes, can I help you?" Bella asked with a slight attitude. She was in her feelings at the moment because of Quavon.

"Shorty, look, I don't got no game. All that rhyming words and shit, my pops ain't never teach me that part of the game. He was too busy chasing them rocks with his clucka ass. On his Pookie shit." Bella burst out laughing at Ace's funny, but yet serious approach. "What's good, beautiful? My name Ace," Ace greeted, sticking his hand out.

"Bella," Bella said, shaking Ace's hand softly.

"So now that I know you and you know me, you here by yourself?" Bella looked him over. He was definitely thugged out in his fitted V-neck Polo shirt, and a crispy pair of True Religions that were fitted. Bella could tell Ace was a street nigga as he was covered in ink, but what held her attention was the diamond chain draped around his neck, as well as the rocks on his earlobes. She could tell he was getting to some money.

"Well, I'm actually here with some friends, but maybe you could give me your number and we can get up and go kick it," Bella said, eyeing Ace down in a proactive manner. Ace was taking his phone off his Louis belt when some niggas walked up.

"Bella, let me holla at you real quick," Quavon said, stepping in Bella's personal space. He had caught her talking to the young cat when he walked up.

"What do you want, Quavon?" Bella was oozing with attitude toward Quavon.

"You ain't gone to introduce me to your little friend?" Quavon asked her, eying Ace down with malice intent. Ace peeped it.

"You know me from somewhere, fam?" Ace said, directing his question to Quavon. It wasn't until Quavon turned towards him to address his statement that Ace saw the G.B.C. chain that hung to the middle of Quavon's chest. He knew he was now in the presence of the infamous Get It Boy Clique. Quavon whispered something in Bella's ear and she mean-mugged him and walked off. Choppa stepped to the side of his boss.

"Check this out, fam. The girl you were just talking is off limits. Shorty bad for your health."

"I respect that, my nigga. I don't beef about no hoes. But I will war over that money," Ace said, throwing some bait out there, trying to catch a shark. Quavon gave him a once over. It looked to him as if Ace was in the streets hustling.

"What you are willing to go to war over and what you not, is none of my concern. So, don't pop that money war shit with me. Nigga, this my city, you better show some respect," Quavon hissed. Ace used this time to show diplomacy. He was thinking on a bigger level.

"I was told respect is something that must be earned. And the way you just spoke to me and came at me with all this gangsta shit, lets me know you don't have a clue who you talking to. But I'ma take that on the chin and chalk it up to your ignorance. But look, big homie, me and my people looking for a plug on them bricks of defense. We got that money. That beef ain't 'bout nothing," Ace said. Quavon laughed in his face.

"Man, let's get the fuck away from this clown ass nigga. This nigga probably the feds," Quavon told his men before they all walked off, leaving Ace standing there, all except Rockett. Rockett was a hustler and he looked at Ace as an opportunity to get some clientele. He had a few kilos of heroin put up in the cut and this was a financial opportunity that he was going to take advantage of.

"When you are ready to do business, hit this number, shawty." Rockett gave Ace a piece of paper with his cellphone number on it. Ace smiled as he accepted the paper. Quavon and the Get It Boy Clique were heavyweights in the streets and the new head, just became a potential lick. His mind started to become criminally activated. He didn't like Quavon or his aura, which only added fuel to the fire.

"Who was them niggas?" KI asked, walking up with Goon.

"That's them G.B.C. niggas, some niggas who about to get they shit split to the white meat," Ace replied.

"Okay then, talk to 'em then," KI said ready to get active, taking a sip from her bottle of Cîroc.

An hour later, the concert was over. Blue Cheese had only performed four songs and CK-30 had performed two of his own tracks. The Homicide Crew stood up congregating when CK-30 walked up with two exotic looking redbones.

"Ace, what's good, my nigga? Y'all enjoy the show?"

"Ain't no secret, my dude. That 'Drop My Op' was that work. Had a nigga on mode. Straight up!" Ace bragged.

"That's what's up. Appreciate the love and support, but check it out, let me rap with you real quick. Y'all two wait for me in the lobby," CK-30 said to the two females that accompanied him. The two chicks walked off, leaving the two men to have some privacy. CK-30 looked at the face on his Audemar Piguet.

"Look, Ace. Give us about two hours then y'all come in there and do what y'all do. Here is the card key to the room, my nigga." Ace took the card and put it in his pocket.

"Don't trip. Just be on point," Ace said as he went off to go holler at the rest of T.H.C. It was time to lace up their boots and go to work.

Inside the exclusive sixteenth floor hotel suite at the Congress Hotel, platinum-selling recording artist, Blue Cheese attended the after party that CK-30 had booked him for, for six grand, which he knew he would get back. A pound of strawberry Kush and boxes of Philly blunts littered the glass table. At another table, a few chicks leaned over a pile of cocaine, getting their sniff on. CK-30 held a bottle of 1738 in one hand and a fat blunt of loud in his other hand. Blue Cheese's music banged through the Bose surround sound system inside the room.

The after party was lit. Blue Cheese's security was all being entertained by the women CK-30 had provided, everything was going smoothly, until the door opened and four masked individuals entered the room, pointing guns and ordering everybody to lay face down on the floor.

"Everybody on the floor. This a robbery. We want money, drugs and jewelry, let's not turn this to a homicide." Omega sneered from behind his ski mask, his hand holding a Glock .40 that he pointed in Blue Cheese's face, at the same time relieving him of the diamonds on his neck. Everyone was robbed for all of their possessions at gunpoint. A Gucci bag filled with two thousand in cash, a few million in jewelry, and four pistols were also taken off the waistlines of a few of Blue Cheese's security detail.

"Tie 'em up," Omega commanded his crew. Ace went in his Marc Jella hoodie to retrieve some plastic zip ties. Goon followed suit. Blue Cheese and his small entourage was zip tied with their hands behind their backs. The females were also tied up, and CK-30 was the last to get secured. Ace gave him a wink from behind the mask.

"We gone find out who you niggas is and when we do, we gone came back down here and get at you, fuck duck ass niggas!" one of Blue Cheese's men threatened in his strong southern accent. Ace took this as an opportunity to let his 'G' shine. Walking up on the man who made the threat, Ace pointed his FNH pistol in his direction and pulled the trigger. The gun's light recoil was almost nonexistent as the 5.62 slug found a home in the dude's back.

"Just know when Y'all come back, don't come talking, come bustin, because as you can see the Chi-Raq and that's what we do down here," Ace growled before he shot the man again, putting him all the way down. Homicide.

"Come on, fam, let's slide," Omega said, tossing the Gucci bag over his shoulder, before him and his goons made their exit from the crime scene, leaving the Florida boys stripped of their money, jewels and one of their men's life taken. And Blue Cheese vowing to never to do a show in Chicago ever again.

Come on, sis, let's get up outta here!" Ace yelled excitedly, jumping in the back seat of the Cadillac truck along with Omega, Goon and Marcus. KI waited until all four of her brothers were in the truck, before she calmly pulled out of the parking lot of the Congress Hotel.

"That was some dumb ass shit! Why you pop buddy like that? Causing all that undue heat." Omega questioned Ace for his reckless behavior.

"Man, fuck that nigga. He should have thought about that shit before he got to popping all that killa shit. Niggas gone respect my murder game out here."

Omega just shook his head as he sunk low in the passenger seat of the Escalade. Chicago police swarmed into the parking lot, just as KI pulled out. The Homicide Crew had just pulled a profitable caper and gotten away with it. The morale they needed was given and the reign of terror they were unleashing would be historic in the streets of Chicago for years to come.

CHAPTER 17

Quavon looked down at his feet at the two large duffle bags containing three point two million dollars of hard-earned street money. He had gotten up with Bank Roll Buddy after Bella kept pressuring him to invest his paper in the diamond game with Bank Roll Buddy and Frank. It was odd to him that Bella was so adamant about him making a move, which raised his suspicion, but he didn't stay thinking about it. All Quavon wanted to do was make a quick flip. He was doing good with the heroin and cocaine Castilino was supplying him with, but to make ten million off of three point two mil was like heaven. In a couple of moves, he could get up a hundred million in no time and at that point, he would retire from the game. Bella walked in the living room, wearing only a thong and Christian Louboutins on her feet.

"What's wrong, baby?" she asked Quavon, rubbing her manicured hands over his three-sixty waves. After the Blue Cheese concert, her and Quavon had a big argument once they got back to the room. Quavon had put her in her place about being all in the nigga's face at the concert. After the heated argument, they ended up having steamy sex, before Quavon took her to O'Hare Airport and sent her back to Tampa, Florida.

"Everything is all good. I'm just hoping I'm making the right decision, giving this cracker my cash like this," Quavon said, looking into the open duffle bags at the stacks of dead white men staring him in his face. Bella sat her voluptuous ass cheeks on his lap, her Juicy Couture perfume invaded his space as she put her arms around his neck, looking him in his eyes.

"Quavon, this is a good move for us, baby. It's going to put you in a different tax bracket. That's going to open up a lot of doors for you," Bella said, before she planted a soft kiss on his lips. Quavon could taste the cherry MAC lip gloss that coated her full lips. He and his girl were caught up in a passionate lip lock until Quavon's iPhone rang. Looking at the caller ID, he saw it was Bank Roll Buddy.

"Yo," Quavon answered.

"Where are you, Quavon? We have to be on time and on point for when Frank arrives. He's the type that doesn't play games."

"Alright. Just chill, white boy. I was on my way out the crib, until you just called. I'm on my way." Quavon ended the call. "Baby, I'm a call you in a minute when I get done handling this business and let you know how everything went." Quavon kissed Bella before he grabbed the two duffle bags full of cash and got en route to meet up with Bank Roll Buddy.

Bella looked out the bedroom window, watching Quavon put the duffle bags of money in the trunk of his Lexus ES 300. A smile came across her lips as she grabbed the phone and dialed a number. The phone rang three times before somebody answered. "The target is en route he should be at the location momentarily," Bella said. Not waiting for a response, Bella ended the call and tossed her phone in the bed. She hated what was about to happen. She had caught feelings for Quavon, but in her field, feelings had no place.

Quavon slid the Lexus through the streets of Tampa Nipsey Hussle's "Hustle and Motivate" pounded through his speakers. Quavon had a funny feeling inside his stomach but ignored it. Quavon was at a red light on OBT Road when he looked in his rearview mirror and saw a black Denali truck that he noticed had been tailing him for five minutes. Quavon was from Chi-Raq, so he wasn't green and was always on point. Quavon pulled off. Making a left on MLK, Quavon saw Denali make the same left.

"Fuck, this nigga following me?" Quavon thought out loud, at the same time activating his stash spot. He grabbed the compact Glock .26 handgun from the stash and placed it on his lap as he turned into a Shell gas station, parking beside a gas pump. Looking in his rearview mirror, he saw the Denali truck cruise by slowly, passing the gas station.

"Faking ass niggas!" Quavon said, putting the Glock back into the stash before he pulled back into traffic.

Ten minutes later, Quavon pulled into the lot of the furniture warehouse where he was supposed to meet up with Bank Roll Buddy. Parking his whip, Quavon looked around the empty parking lot, trying to locate Bank Roll Buddy's Benz, but came up blank.

Quavon grabbed his iPhone of his Hermes belt and was about to call him, until four SUVs stormed into the parking lot, coming to a screeching halt behind Quavon's Lexus, boxing him in. Quavon thought it was jack boys until he saw the red and blue lights flashing inside the grills of the trucks. The doors flung open and men jumped out, pointing Glocks at Quavon's whip.

"Driver, turn the ignition off and drop your keys out the window with your right hand and step out of the vehicle," Quavon heard over the bullhorn. He could see the dark blue jacket with bold yellow letters on them that read, "U.S. Marshals."

"Fuck," Quavon cursed himself for not following his gut instinct. Taking the keys out the ignition, he obliged to the officer's command and dropped the keys out the window. When Quavon was about to attempt to get out of the car, one of the U.S. Marshals rushed the Lexus and violently yanked open the driver's side door and aggressively grabbed Quavon by his Polo V-neck shirt and forced him to the concrete.

"Hands behind your back, asshole," the Marshal barked, slapping the cold cuffs on Quavon's wrists.

After being thoroughly pat searched, Quavon was put inside of an unmarked Crown Victoria, where he sat witnessing the feds tear apart the Lexus. They popped the trunk to retrieve the two duffle bags full of dope money. A couple of officers gave each other high fives, after examining the contents of the bags. Quavon gritted his teeth as he thought about Bank Roll Buddy setting him up with the feds. He made a vow to himself that once he made it out, he was going to kill Bank Roll Buddy personally.

Quavon was escorted to a federal holding facility in downtown Tampa, Florida. He was sitting in a cold holding cell when he heard a voice that shattered his heart into in a million pieces.

"Quavon Anderson, I'm Agent Hernandez. You have anything you want to talk to us about, pertaining to your criminal activity in Chicago?" Quavon couldn't believe the voice he just heard, looking up only to see Bella. His blood started to boil instantly and the love he once held for Bella was now replaced by pure hatred.

"Bitch. All this time I been sleeping with the fucking feds? You rat scum bucket bitch!" Quavon hissed before he spit in Bella's face through the jail bars. Bella wiped the thick gook off her face with the back of her hand. To say she was embarrassed would be an understatement.

"Oh, you can add assaulting a federal agent to your indictment too, you drug dealer, small-minded, lil dick ass boy," Agent Hernandez said out of emotion, while Agent Robert Johnson walked up. Quavon couldn't believe his eyes. Bank Roll Buddy had been the feds the whole time.

What Quavon didn't know was that he was the target of a federal money laundering investigation and Agent Johnson was leading a pack of wolves. The two of them had been partners for the past ten years and had been running the same sting operation, catching a lot of big money heavyweights. The feds didn't care about niggas getting money, just as long as Uncle Sam got his cut. The feds knew about Quavon and his drug dealing in Chicago. But to get money and not share the wealth would be unacceptable, so the investigation was launched.

"You know, Mr. Anderson, you are in a position to help yourself. All we want is to know who your wholesale drug supplier is," Agent Johnson said, trying to get Quavon to snitch. This was a test of his manhood.

"I want my lawyer," Quavon replied as he manned up. Agent Hernandez laughed.

"You don't remember all those talks we had when we was laid up, right after I put this bomb pussy on your tiny little moustache. You shot this nigga this and that. You know, all the things you and your gang banging buddies doing in Chicago, but guess what? All these conversations were recorded, sweetheart, so it would be in your best interest to cooperate with the government under the 5-K-1. We can let you back in the streets."

Agent Hernandez watched Quavon rub his goatee as if he was pondering what she was speaking on. She knew she had him right where she wanted him. He had told her so much about what he was involved in, his name was open and she knew it. "So, what is going to be, Quavon?"

"You funky cock bitch. You didn't hear what I said the first time. If you didn't, let me tell your rat ass again, go get my lawyer," Quavon growled.

"Very well, just know I'm going to do everything in my power to make sure you get no less than three hundred and sixty months... thirty years. Maybe you will end up at the same prison as your big brother, Yaton," Agent Hernandez threatened before she and Agent Johnson walked off.

Quavon knew if he fed ten percent of the shit he talked to Bella about, that's a done deal. He had gone against the main rule YaYo had told him about, silence and secrecy. Quavon never spoke on the Nation's business to any non-member. Now he had just got popped for violating the most important law of all.

Two days later, Quavon had his first initial court date. He was indicted on one count of money laundering. The magistrate judge gave Quavon a fifty-thousand-dollar cash bond. Quavon hated jail, he would have given every red penny up for him not to send another night in jail. Karen, Quavon's mom, was on her way to Tampa from Orlando. She posted her son's bail. She had to put up the beauty salon up as collateral, so she could take out a secure loan from the bank.

Quavon thought about asking his pops Darrell to post his bail, but thought against it. He could resort to reaching out to the Get It Boy Clique, but he knew the feds were on his back. Quavon had just taken a big loss and the fact was, he was in the red with the plug, Castilino. Quavon had to get out of jail and get back to the grind. His stressing over his situation was broken up when the correctional officer came to the holding cell.

"Quavon Anderson. Pack up, you just made bail," the officer informed him. Quavon got off the cold steel bench he had been lying on. The officer unlocked the cell and stepped to the side to allow Quavon to walk out the cell. After getting processed out of the federal holding facility, Quavon walked out two hours later. He was told he had to report to the M.C.C. Federal Building downtown, where a federal house arrest bracelet would be secured on his ankle to make sure he would make his next court date. After walking out the building, Quavon was surprised to see his parents standing in front of the jail waiting for him.

"Thanks, Mama," Quavon said, walking up and embracing his mother.

"Baby, is everything alright? Some agent called me talking about you would be going to prison about some drug stuff and if I knew anything about it, you would be put in something called a conspiracy. Quavon, what these white folks talking about? I'm starting to get worried," Karen said into her son's chest as she held him. Quavon looked in his mother's face, holding her shoulders, making sure he had her attention.

"Mama, listen, don't worry. I'm going to fix this situation, it's just a mix-up my lawyer is going to fix. Don't worry, they are just trying to stress you because they have nothing on me. But we will talk about his later, okay?" Quavon said, trying to keep the conversation short in front of his father. This was his first time seeing his father since he stepped back in the picture. He didn't want his father in any of his business. Quavon got out of his mother's embrace and walked over to his father.

"What's good, Pops?" Quavon greeted. Darrell looked Quavon up and down before he spoke.

"So, you turned out to be a lil street nigga, huh?"

"Naw, I turned out to be a boss. But continue," Quavon said, giving his father the floor. Darrell laughed slightly.

"Quavon... listen, son. I didn't come here to have a pissing match with you, I came because your mother wanted me to come. You are a grown man now, to make your own decisions. You know right from wrong, Quavon. Nobody is going to baby you. You in the game now, but guess what? I'm giving you some game. You need to take heed to when you are involved in something, no matter what it is. Make sure you do your homework and know what you are a part of, because you might have to die for it."

Quavon looked into his father's eyes. "I appreciate the game, Pops, but I got everything under control. Thanks for just dropping me and Davon off in Chicago like that too. That was real caring on your behalf. And to not pop up until years later? That shows signs of a good parent," Quavon said sarcastically. "Now if you don't mind, I have a plane to catch back to Chicago. I have a lot of shit to do," Quavon said, getting into the backseat of his mother's Trailblazer.

Darrell just shook his head. Quavon's words cut him like a knife, just as YaYo's words had. His guilt was evident as he just lowered his head. He had destroyed two lives because of his jealousy and physical abuse. His bogus parenting had destroyed YaYo and Quavon's lives. He should have never sent them to Chicago at such young ages, knowing the streets would swallow them whole and would spit them out as savages.

Thirty minutes later, Quavon was at the Tampa International Airport. Quavon had already booked his flight by phone. As he was getting out the truck, Karen and Darrell also got out to see their son off.

"Okay, man. I'm a call you when I get home."

"Okay, son. You make sure you do and be safe out there, Quavon."

"Don't worry about me. Everything will be alright. I promise." Quavon kissed his mother on her cheek. "Alright, Pops, you be cool, make sure Moms is good."

"Alright, son. Make the right decision as a man. Man up, and take care of your responsibilities," Darrell said. He would just keep Quavon in his prayers and hope his hard head wouldn't be the cause of his ruin. Quavon nodded his head and made his way inside the airport. Trials and tribulations were ahead of him, so he had to utilize his five P's: *Proper preparation prevents poor performance.* Quavon had to play offense and he needed to set his priorities together. He'd just lost three point two million and he definitely had to get that back. Until then, niggas was gone feel his wrath.

CHAPTER 18

WGN NEWS

"On today's top story, Florida recording artist Blue Cheese was the victim of a violent robbery. His bodyguard was shot to death at the Congress Hotel downtown, after his concert that was held at the United Center. Witnesses say the rapper was attending the after party when four men, armed with handguns, entered the hotel room demanding jewelry and money. One person was killed in the robbery. Authorities have no suspects at the time and would like anybody with information on this violent crime to notify the Chicago police."

We made the news, my nigga!" Ace said, geeked up. He had just watched the news on his iPhone. The Homicide Crew was at a hotel room in Gary, Indiana, right outside of Chicago. They had a pound of loud that they were smoking on and bottles of Cîroc being passed around the room. The robbers came out to sixty-two thousand in cash and six million worth of ice.

"Aye check, family." Ace said, getting everybody's attention, he picked back up his phone. Tying a white t-Shirt around the lower half of his face logged onto Facebook and went live and turned the phone to himself.

"This is your boy, Homicide Ace. This is a message from The Homicide Crew. If you doing a brick or better, I suggest you keep that shit on the low, because we want our cut. You bitch niggas either cut us in, or cut it out. That go for entertainers as well. Ask Blue Cheese didn't we send him back to Miami naked and afraid. Pussy ass niggas, these our streets. Aye yo... Blue Cheese, appreciate it, fam. Get at us if you want it back. Homicide Crew, niggas!" Ace yelled in the phone before he logged off.

"Man, you dumb as hell," Omega said, thumbing through a large wad of American currency.

"Fuck what you talking about, it's time to let these niggas out here know what time it is. Either get down or lay down," Ace retorted, standing on his gangsta.

"Anyway nigga. What's up with them G.B.C. niggas that had you cornered off?" KI said, joking with Ace as she split a cigar in half to fill it with weed.

"Niggas ain't have me cornered shit. On Ray Ray," Ace said, putting it on his dead homie taking KI's joke offensive.

"Boy, I'm just playing with your soft ass. On some serious shit, what's up with niggas?"

"The nigga who ran them named Quavon. He was on some arrogant shit because his hoe was on my dick."

"Who is his bitch?" KI questioned.

"I don't know, some bitch named Bella. But anyway, I sent the hook out there about copping some work. He curve balled that bitch, said some slick shit and walked off, but one of his men stayed back to holler at me. He told me when I was ready to holler at him, he gave me his contact information," Ace said, remembering the conversation he had with Rockett.

"So, you think it's sweet or what, Ace?" KI wanted more info on the lick.

"Hell yeah, it's sweet. I gufrued suggest we shop with them niggas. About three times, then sting him for the last one and you already know we gone have to kill 'em."

"Ain't no question, he's gotta go. That ain't what I'm worried about. I'm just tying to see how much this nigga worth. Ain't no sense in playing with these niggas, if they got it, we want it," Omega intervened. He wanted everything Rockett was holding.

"Matter of fact, let me show you how I'm a rock this nigga to sleep." Ace got his cell phone. Searching his contact list, he found what he was looking for and called the number.

"Who dis, shawty?" Rockett's southern drawl came over the line.

"This Ace. I met you at the Blue Cheese concert."

"Oh, what's good, shawty? How you living?"

"I'm good, I'm living but could I be living a lil better, feel me?"

"That's a bet. But look, I'm a call you back in thirty minutes. Stay close to your phone."

"Alright, say less," was Ace's only reply before he ended the call.

"What does he say, lil bro?" Goon asked.

"He said he would call me back in about thirty minutes." Thirty minutes later, Ace's phone rang.

"Speak on it, family," Ace answered, already knowing it was Rockett on the other line.

"Aye shawty, meet me at Pepe's so we can eat a lil something and talk business.

"Alright, I'll meet you there."

"See you in a minute, shawty" Rockett ended the call.

"Aye, check it out, y'all. I'm about to meet this nigga at the Mexican spot, Pepe's. Goon, you trail me in the Hellcat, just in case this nigga on some bullshit, we'll be in position to nail his goofy ass and get away with it."

"Tell that nigga we got thirty racks we trying to spend with him on the first demonstration." Omega said.

"Omega, chill your baldhead ass down, nigga. I told you I got this," Ace replied, arrogant as hell.

"Man, just handle the business, Ace, and quit talking shit." Omega was starting to become irritated with Ace. Ace was his man, but a time like this, he wanted Ace to be on point and on his A-game. Militant mind frame.

Later on that night, Ace sat across the booth from Rockett at the Pepe's Mexican restaurant on the south side. They ordered burritos and two cold pitchers of Corona beer.

"So, you said you are trying to spend three-fifty?" Rockett asked, taking a bite from his chicken and steak burrito.

You know, anywhere in the Midwest, niggas charging eighty to eighty-five a brick and a lot of nigga's shit even taking more than three on the cut side."

"So how much do you like your work taking?"

"My dope taking six. You know I'm hustling on the west side, so I gotta keep my shit legit. Too much competition to be trying to sell garbage, shawty."

"No doubt, No doubt," Ace said, like he was in complete understanding and compliance to what Rockett was kicking. Ace knew Rockett was overtaking him on the dope, but Ace couldn't care less. He was baking Rockett a cake anyway.

"Listen, this what I'm a do for you shawty, since this is the first time we doing business. To show you in good hands, for your three hundred and fifty geez, I'm going to give you five bricks of some work you can cut six times. The more money you bring, the cheaper the prices get. You understand, shawty?"

"That's all love, my nigga. I'm ready to get active. When are you ready for me?" Ace said, ready to get the ball rolling.

"Get the bread right and stay by the phone, shawty."

"Say less, my nigga," Ace replied. The two continued to eat their meals until it was time to handle the business. Ace left to get the paper right and Rockett went to go handle what needed to be handled to supply Ace's order.

Rockett put the last kilo in the duffle bag before zipping it up, putting its strap over his shoulder. Checking the clip to his Glock .357, seeing it had twelve hollow point rounds in the magazine, he stuck the mag into the handle of the Glock and pulled the slide back, putting one in the chamber. He put the gun in the front pocket of his jacket, leaving the trap house where he had a brick of heroin and cocaine stashed. Nobody knew about the spot. Not even Choppa was aware of the spot. And that's how Rockett wanted to keep it.

He had been cuffing bricks of dope from the G.B.C. since the score on Castilino's truck. In his mind, he wasn't taking anything he didn't deserve. The fact of the matter was that Rockett was starting to feel like a piece of shit for letting Quavon kill his Blood family. His mother was still grieving over her brother's murder and it made him feel like shit.

Rockett really didn't trust Quavon as he knew the young gangster was unpredictable, which was a dangerous, deadly habit to have and he could easily become his enemy. Rockett wanted to be ready physically and mentally when the time came when he would have to take Quavon and the G.B.C. to war. Until then, he would just play his position as a soldier and bust his moves on the side to get his weight up.

Rockett left the trap and got in his lowkey Dodge Charger. He placed the bag in the backseat and pulled out of the driveway to go meet up with Ace.

"Fuck copping from this nigga two or three times. Bust him for the six bricks."

"You sure, fam?" Ace asked Omega, putting the last ten-stack bundle into the Gucci luggage bag.

"Yeah, I'm sure, Ace. This nigga janky anyway, he sneaking around doing shit behind his people back. Bust 'em for the six," Omega said. Ace looked at KI, then Goon and then Marcus.

"Man, I ain't trippin, it's whatever y'all want to do," Goon spoke up for the first time.

"What about you, KI?" Ace asked.

"I agree with Omega, we hit him for the bricks he about to bring, ain't no sense playing games with this nigga. The more times he meets up with Ace, the more familiar he would become with him and the more of opportunity of something going wrong, feel me?" Ace thought about KI's logic and it made sense to him. So, he opted to go with his team's recommendations on how the lick would go.

"Alright, I'm rolling with y'all on this one. This the business. I'm a meet this nigga on 39th and Prairie, across from Wendell Phillips High School. I jump in the car with him with the money. Goon, you and Marcus be parked at the stop sign at the corner. He got to come past y'all. When he stops at the stop sign, jump out and nail buddy ass. Make sure that nigga all the way out. Hit him in the head a couple times, because we don't need no fuck ups," Ace commanded. He was young but when it came down to murder, he was a general. And his crew knew it.

Rockett sat on the seat of his Dodge Charger. Ace was ten minutes late and Rockett was starting to get antsy, until he saw the headlights coming down Prairie Street. The car was creeping down the block slowly. It was 8:30 at night and the block was remotely empty. The car coming up to him flashed its headlights. Rockett did the same, signaling him to park in front of his whip in which he did.

Ace grabbed the duffle bag from the back seat and got out his vehicle and jumped in the Charger with Rockett.

"What's good, shawty, everythang, everythang?" Rockett asked, his head on survival, checking his surroundings.

"Yes, everything all well," Ace replied by unzipping the duffle bag full of blue notes. Rockett got the bag and examined what laid inside.

"I don't have to count this, do I, shawty?"

"You gone do what you gone do, fam. I don't play no games, my nigga, because I don't want a nigga playing with me, feel me?" Ace retorted.

"I can dig it, shawty. Your stuff is in the backseat." Ace reached in the backseat for the backpack, unzipping it to show six neatly wrapped kilos of heroin. Ace zipped the bag back up, satisfied with its contents.

"I guess that concludes our business right now. I'm a get at your fam when I get done dumping this shit. Give me a few weeks," Ace said, reaching for the door handle.

"Get at me when you ready, shawty." Ace jumped back in his whip and pulled off, going one way down Prairie Street Rockett going the opposite way down Prairie Street.

"Here go this nigga right here," Goon said from the passenger seat of the bubble Chevy Caprice. He grabbed the FN pistol from under the seat and pulled the ski mask over his face, just as Rockett pulled up to the stop sign. Rockett was looking at his iPhone when the first shot shattered his windshield. The rapid gunshots that barked from the FN broke the silence of the quiet block.

Rockett felt nothing as a slug hit him in his temple, putting his brain on the dashboard. Goon opened the driver's side door and continued to shoot Rockett until he was out of ammunition. Twenty 5.62 rounds had been fired, with thirteen of them hitting Rockett's body. The killer reached inside the Charger and grabbed the duffle bag full of cash, before hopping back in the Caprice. They pulled off, leaving Rockett's brains splattered all in his whip. His body was added to Chicago's high murder rate.

CHAPTER 19

Fifty-nine, fifty-eight, fifty-seven, fifty-six... YaYo counted in his head while he did his burpees. The only clothing he wore was two pairs of boxers and a pair of socks. YaYo was facing the cell door, working out in the small cell. This was part of his daily routine. His celly Nino laid on his bunk, no shirt, just boxers. The heat was scorching inside the cell. It was the middle of the summer in Pennsylvania and Lewisburg Penitentiary had no AC or central air. No ventilation at all. The only air circulating in the prison was the large fans at the end of each tier.

Most inmates would lay on the floor in front of the cell door so they could catch some of the air coming from the hallway. Lewisburg Penitentiary was a hundred years old and one of the oldest prisons in the Bureau. Living conditions at Lewisburg was close to hellacious. YaYo didn't let the steamy heat break him like it did most inmates. Instead, he embraced it. Working out in the extreme temperature worked in his favor as he was able to shred body fat and sculpt his frame viciously, giving him the body of a personal trainer.

He had been in the S.M.U. now for ten months and was on the second phase of the programs. In eight more months, he would be leaving Lewisburg to be transferred to a different USP. YaYo had transitioned into the S.M.U. well. He used his time wisely to study the Quran, work out, as well as write. YaYo had found his true passion in life. And that was storytelling. He had finished his manuscript called *Drill Season* and was now working on Part 3 of *Trilogy*. YaYo had cut his long dreads, now he sported a murda one...baldhead with a goatee.

Being in the cell with Nino had also proved to be a blessing. Nino was a scholar and he was the student.. Nino was smart, educated and full of game. Nino schooled YaYo on many subjects, such as politics, crime, how to build your credit, and business management skills. YaYo was in the cell with a boss.

He was also getting a lot of mail from his daughter Shamira. In every letter, YaYo would give her some kind of knowledge, wisdom and understanding. Shamira was only five years old, but he schooled her like she was older. He missed his daughter so much and couldn't wait to be back out there with her. YaYo had given his baby mama Shakira the authority to take over the shop since his mom had moved to Florida. She was doing well, conducting the business and had even started to get more clients at Style and Grace. He knew he had made the right decision in purchasing the salon. It was a boss move.

Over the last ten months, he also watched Jamari grow up from pictures. The more pictures Ms. Sanchez sent him of the little boy, the more YaYo knew that Jamari was his own. His features were starting to flourish and Jamari had identical features like Shamira. YaYo dreaded the day he had to tell Shikira about Ms. Sanchez and Jamari. It would crush his wife. But she would have to know if he wanted to be a father to his son.

After completing his workout, YaYo placed some cleaning solution over the puddles of sweat on the floor. Grabbing the floor towel, he wiped up the mess he had caused. After cleaning the cell, YaYo tied a sheet from his mattress to the vent and tied it to the end of the bunk, separating the boxed cell by the sheet so he could have some privacy. YaYo washed up using the sink and put on some fresh boxers and socks, then climbed back up on his bunk to allow Nino to have some floor time.

The cell was so small, two grown men could not stand up and move around the cell at the same time. YaYo and Nino took turns working out. When one was done, then the other would get up to do his mandatory workout. You had to find some way to release your energy being locked in the small closet for twenty-three hours out of the day.

After they had both worked out and took care of their hygiene, YaYo and Nino sat in the cell conversating as they usually do.

"You know, eight months is no time….It's that time that will sneak up on you, especially from where you come from in the feds and what you have been through. What's your plans for when you bounce, Ock?" Nino asked out of nowhere. He wanted YaYo to plan for the future and always think ahead, because a man with no plan, only plans to fail, Nino would always preach to YaYo.

"You already know, Nino. I'm about to try and push these books I've been writing, start my own publishing company and once I get my bag up, I'm a get me a weed dispensary. I know what I want to do," YaYo said, with his morale high about the goals he wanted to achieve in life. When it came to hustling, the entire city of Chicago knew YaYo was that nigga.

As a teenager, YaYo held the character of a dictator, as he and his men controlled the drug trade in the Midwest region. And he knew if he wanted, once he got released, he could get right back in the streets and control it with an iron fist, but YaYo was adamant about the promise he made to Mr. B.

Mr. B was the reason he was going to be released in a few years. Had it not been for Mr. B, YaYo would've died behind the walls of a maximum federal penitentiary, that he was sure of. So, he was going to stand on his word as a man. YaYo was going to do all in his power to bring about peace in the streets of Chicago. How, he did not have the slightest idea.

"YaYo, I see you know what you want to do, but do you know how to go about doing it? Listen, YaYo, the key to getting what you want in life, is to act as if you already have it. It's called the power of your subconscious mind, and what that is, is basically in your mind you already have what you desire. That positive energy is circulated into the universe and comes back around to you in the three-hundred-sixty-degree circle of life.

And it comes back to you because it was you who put it out here. And always remember, YaYo, to plan to the end in whatever endeavor you choose. Write your goals down and achieve them, then make sure your goals are realistic, specific and time bound. Trust me, this shit work, Ock," Nino schooled, dropping precious life changing jewels on YaYo. YaYo just sat back on his bunk, digesting the game Nino had just given him, as he always did.

"Yeah, you right, Nino, I need to put the clamps down on what I'm trying to do. It's crunch time. I want to finish four more books before I go home. I know when I get to the compound, I'm going to have a lot of running around to do."

"See, that's what I'm saying, YaYo... Stop rushing into things, running around on the yard is one of the reasons that landed you in S.M.U. Remember this, if you don't remember anything else I ever told you, if it's not conducive to your future then it should hold not one minute of your attention," Nino said, hoping YaYo saw the point that he was trying to make.

The next day, YaYo and Nino were in the recreation cage, doing some Navy Seals. An extreme push, considering it was a hundred and ten degrees, and the heat was the enemy as YaYo hopped down to do his set. Two more inmates occupied the cage besides YaYo and Nino. They were two of the homies from Chicago. One's name was Dread. He was a Black Soul gang member from the west side of Chicago, serving life in prison for conspiracy to sell ten kilograms of Fentanyl. The other inmate's name was Lil G. He was from the north side of the city and had fifteen years for a stash house case.

"Come on, Nino. It's your count, old head," YaYo said, while waiting for Nino to go down on his set. Nino was bent over with his hands on his knees, trying to catch his breath.

"Come on, Gangsta, ain't no timeout on the battlefield. Let's go!" YaYo said, jogging in place.

"Man, I'm tapped out, fam," Nino replied and took a seat in the back of the recreation cage. YaYo continued to get money, finishing the workout.

Two hundred Navy Seals later, YaYo had completed the workout. Sweat poured from his chiseled body. YaYo had come a long way since he had come to the feds. He was never a skinny dude, but now he had cut muscles, a six-pack and his body was now covered in ink, he definitely had the federal goon look.

"Aye YaYo, check it out real quick, homie," Hector said from the next cage. Hector was a southern California Mexican. His gang affiliation was Sureño. The Sureño's in the S.M.U. was in alliance with the MS-13 gang members, as well as the Pisas. Their enemies were the northern California Mexicans. The Norteño's gang was their rivals. It was an on-sight war between the two gangs and Lewisburg was a battleground for them. The Sureño's really don't mess with blacks, but YaYo and Nino had a mutual respect for each other. YaYo walked to the side of the cage where Hector was.

"What's good, Hector? How are you?"

"Good, my friend. I was told to bring this out to you." Hector discreetly slid YaYo a small folded piece of paper with tape on it. "It comes from your homie downstairs on the first floor. He said give it to you or your celly. I mess with you, so you who I gave it to," Hector said. YaYo slid the piece of paper between the lining of his pants.

"Appreciate you, Hector," YaYo thanked him.

"No problem, ese."

Back inside of their cell, YaYo and Nino had taken turns bathing in the sink inside of the cell. It was called a bird bath for convicts. In the S.M.U., you were only allowed three showers a week, so in order to stay fresh and clean, you had to use the sink. YaYo sat on the bunk and got the note Hector had given him in the rec cage. Opening it, he began to read. What he read made his eyes bulge.

"Ain't no way! Listen y'all, the nigga y'all in the rec cage with named Lil G, he from the North side. Howard and Damen—they call their hood the jungle! That nigga Lil G a rat, he told on a nigga about a body in South Carolina and that's a fact." YaYo finished reading the scribe out loud to Nino.

"Man, this nigga the police and we got his jake ass around us," YaYo fumed.

"Hold tight, how we know this info is valid? Matter fact, who sent this over here?" Nino said, taking the paper from YaYo and reading it over.

"It doesn't even say who this came from. We don't know nothin about this shit," Nino said, not wanting to jump the gun without any proof.

"But what if he is that? That nigga can't be in the cage with us. And if other niggas knew about this, how that make us look, we got his rat ass in the cage with us. I'm a tell you how it make us look, like we condoning his rat shit. Perception is everything, we can't be showing no weakness around here, fam," YaYo said, taking the memo is a lil more serious than Nino.

"So, what do you suggest we do, YaYo? Say he is hot. Then what? We gonna smash him out in the cage and we only got eight months left till we complete the program. For what? Because a nigga told on a nigga. That's something he have to deal with for the rest of his life, that shit gone catch up with him. I'm trying to get out the S.M.U., and you should too. Fuck that nigga if he is hot," Nino said, knowing where YaYo was trying to take the situation.

"I understand all of that, Nino, but understand this. I was told by a wise man that a solid reputation takes years and years of blood, sweat and tears to obtain, but only one second to destroy. I am protecting my reputation at all costs," YaYo said, standing on principle.

"You do what you have to do, brother," Nino replied.

"I plan to," YaYo retorted and pulled out a book about limited liability companies and started to read. He didn't want to keep going back and forth with Nina about business. If the nigga Lil-G was hot, he was going to have to find a different recreation cage, either by choice or force. YaYo couldn't wait to go to recreation tomorrow. He had an announcement to make.

It was 12:30 the next day when the tall C.O. escorted YaYo to the rec cage for his hour of recreation. Once in the cage, YaYo squatted down so he could stick his hands through the slot so the correctional officer could take off his handcuffs. After the C.O. relieved YaYo of his cuffs, the officer let Nino in the cage and repeated the process. Lil-G and Dread were already in the cage. YaYo walked over and gave both of them some dap, at the same time watching the C.O.'s make their way down the walkway and disappear out of sight.

"Aye everybody, check it out real quick." Lil-G and Dread came over to where YaYo and Nino was standing.

"What up?" Lil-G asked.

"This the business. Everybody need to bring they paperwork out to so we can swap work," YaYo said as he watched the reaction from both of them. Lil-G's reaction was most shocking.

"What I need to bring my work out for? Niggas already know I'm official." YaYo looked at him sideways.

"Man… look fam, we ain't going for no vouching, we need to see that work. If niggas ain't trying to produce they work, then they definitely in the wrong cage. Straight up!" YaYo said, crossing his arms over his broad chest, ready to stand on his word if need be.

"I ain't got no problem showing my work. I'll send mine down the tier when we go back in the building," Lil-G said.

"That's what's up. I'm a fish me and my celly work down there to you. This shit ain't personal, my nigga, we just trying to make sure everybody on the same page and living the same way. You know perception is everything, my niggas," YaYo said. Everybody agreed to show their paperwork and he didn't have to get violent.

"You think he gon' bring that work out next time we got rec? Because he definitely hasn't called down here this year," YaYo asked Nino, once back in the cell.

"He said he was. Let's just be patient and wait and see," Nino responded.

"So, I guess when Monday rolls around and he steps in that cage and he ain't got that work, then I guess we have a decision to make, huh?"

"Yeah, I guess so. 'Cause I ain't gone be in the cage with no Sammy the Bulls, straight up," YaYo vowed. YaYo was focused on getting out the S.M.U. and didn't want to get set back to day one-phase one, but at the same time, he wouldn't bend his morals and principles for nobody. Or no one!

CHAPTER 20

"Man, I don't give a fuck! I'm a shoot every motherfucka I think had something to do with this shit. That's on God!" Choppa vented as he held an FNH handgun in one hand and cradled an AK-47 in the other hand. His eyes were bloodshot red from the countless hours he had been crying after finding out about Rockett's murder. Rockett's homicide had made the WGN News at 9. Police said there was no witnesses to the killing, and the authorities had no leads on the suspects believed to be involved in the violent crime.

Rockett had called Choppa right before he left his spot to go serve Ace, and that's what he told Choppa. Choppa had put ten geez on anybody who knew who Ace was and his location. Choppa remembered seeing Ace's face at the United Center. He stood next to Quavon when he was checking Ace about hollering at his girl, Bella. Ace's face was now sketched in Choppa's mind. Choppa wanted nothing more in life right now then to put a bullet in Ace's head and Choppa vowed that when time presented itself, he would do just that.

"Choppa, just chill, fam. It's a lot of shit going on right now. We got the feds snooping around. These crackers just put a case on me on some bullshit. If we just start dropping bodies in the city, they really gone be on a nigga line. You gotta think, Choppa." Quavon said, pacing back and forth. He was stressing hard. He had just lost three point two million, got a fed case and just found out one of his men had just lost his life. The walls were starting to close in on him. Not to mention, they now had beef with enemies they knew nothing about.

"Choppa, Quavon is right. We can't just go out shooting muthafuckers, we got to do your homework and move strategically. We ain't make it this far by moving recklessly. This shit about longevity," Crusha intervened, trying to get Choppa to see Quavon's logic.

Choppa's heart was beating rapidly, his blood was boiling and he wanted nothin more than to seek revenge on the niggas.

Who just shot his people? What Quavon and Crusha were speaking, went in one ear and out the other. Choppa was ready to shed blood. Tonight, somebody had to die in retribution of his dead homie.

"Crusha, what's our inventory on the bricks we got put up?" Quavon asked, thinking about money. Crusha went in his mental Rolodex.

"We should have a hunnid and sixty bricks of heroin and about thirty bricks of Chico cocaine," Crusha informed his boss. Quavon did the mental math. The G.B.C. was down to their last bricks and they needed to go back across the border to holler at Castilino.

"Listen, Crusha, I need you to get Suge a hunnid of those bricks off D. Tell him we need to get them off as quick as he can. Tell him don't worry about the ticket. Tell 'em I said to weather the storm with us, and we gone hit him on the back end. We need his help. Choppa, I need you to rack up the money we got floating around in the streets. Do what you got to do to get that money back to the house. We gotta get Castilino his money for the bricks we owe for and we short, hella short.

If we don't get that nigga money, then we really gone have a problem when he starts sending them Cartel niggas over here. That's a war we ain't ready to fight," Quavon explained to his men. Choppa was geeked that he got put in charge of collecting G.B.C. drug debts. Now he could unleash some pent-up frustration in the streets of Chicago.

"My niggas, we been in this spot when niggas was gunning at us from every angle of the game. We just handle the business and not let nothing dictate our pace. This shit a dictatorship. Not a democracy. You with me?" Quavon asked his chain of command.

"I'm with whatever demonstration you put down, Quavon. I just feel like Choppa. Them niggas, whoever they are, need to pay for how they left Rockett all shot up like that. They took one of our best shooters and they need to be dealt with. Quickly," Reggie-G said with a broken heart. He had learned to love Rockett as a brother and the pain he was feeling for his death was almost unbearable and he wanted to taste blood.

"Make no mistake about it, Reggie-G. They will be dealt with in a timely fashion, but what I'm trying to get y'all to see is that we got to get this money up, so we can secure the plug. We ain't shit out here in these streets without this paper," Quavon boomed as he tried to get his team to see the importance of money one more time. He got tired of explaining himself. He gave everybody an equal voice within the gang, but he was the undisputed leader of the G.B.C. and what he said was law!

Choppa tucked his FN on his waistline and checked the hunnid-round drum to his AK-47. "I'm about to bounce up outta here. I need some air, and plus I got to handle some nation business. I'm a holler at you niggas in a minute," Choppa said and made his way out the front door. Everybody remaining knew that he was about to go and kill somebody!

"Let's tighten this shit up," Quavon said, walking towards the door with Crusha and Reggie-G in tow. He had some moves to make and he couldn't make them sitting around twiddling his thumbs.

"This hoe is a straight up *thot*! She on a nigga line. I should gone head and nail her lil thick ass. How she look, G?" Half-Pint said, passing his homie Jue-Ball his iPhone11. Jue-Ball looked at the chick's Instagram page on Half-Pint's phone.

"She decent, Scud. I'd fuck her if I was you," Jue-Ball said, passing Pint back his phone. He put it on the clip on his Louis Vuitton belt. Half-Pint and Jue-Ball was G.B.C. gangsters that sold drugs for the G.B.C.

Tonight was just another night on 69th and Wolcott, their block as well as their turf. Six other gang members stood on the corner of Walcott, hustling and smoking blunts. It was a hot summer night and the block was in full swing. Everybody was wondering what they did, when a black Porsche truck with tinted windows turned down Wolcott.

"Who the fuck is that?" Jue-Ball probed as he reached for the handle of his .45 that rested on his waist. The truck parked at the corner where the men was standing. Jue-Ball's gun was now visible at his side. The window rolled down.

"Aye, Half-Pint, check it out real quick," Choppa said in the driver's seat of the Porsche truck. Half-Pint looked around nervously before he walked over to the truck.

"What's good, Choppa?" Half-Pint said, once he got to the passenger side window, where he could see the FN laying across Choppa's lap.

"Ain't shit good with me. What's good with you? You niggas got that bread for them three bricks?" Choppa questioned.

"Naw, not yet. It's been a lil slow out here. As you can see," Half-Pint replied.

"You mean to tell me, you niggas had the work for a month and some change and y'all ain't sold not one bag?" Choppa sneered.

"That's just what it is, fam. We can't make these smokers magically appear."

Choppa let out a slight chuckle before he calmly stepped out of the SUV. He walked up on the curb where Half-Pint stood and brought the FN down on top of his head. His meat split upon contact of the large handgun. Half-Pint fell to his knees, but Choppa held him by his black tee to prevent him from falling down on the concrete as he rained blow upon blow upside his skull, fracturing it in many places. Choppa pistol whipped Half-Pint until he was laid out unconscious on the corner of 69th and Wolcott.

Out of breath, Choppa tucked the bloody handgun back on his waist. "You get this smart mouth ass nigga to a hospital, and when he able to walk and talk again, put him on the security detail since his money management skills fucked up. Until further notice, Jue-Ball, you in charge of the block and making sure that money is right. When I swing back through here, that money better be right, or somebody gone be made an example of. Don't let it be you," Choppa threatened, eyeing Jue-Ball as he got back in the Porsche truck.

A nigga had just put their hands on an elite G.B.C. member, which meant niggas was in the streets starting to get comfortable. The wolves were packing up because they now smelled blood. The streets were definitely watching and waiting for a response from the G.B.C. Their retaliation had to be swift and vicious; Choppa was aware of that. So, to show his alliance to his gang and his belief in their politics, Choppa would forever have blind loyalty to the Get It Boy Clique.

"Alright, thanks a lot, Ted. I really appreciate your time. You bet. Take it easy, pal," Detective Jones said, putting the phone back on the cradle. He was at his desk at the 51st Precinct, going over some notes when he got the call he had been waiting for. Detective Jones had Marcus's DNA taken off the Glock he got caught with tested in the National Databank and unexpectedly, it came up in a match related to a crime in Somerville, Tennessee, in which that crime was a homicide.

"Aye Flowers. you ain't gonna believe this shit, partner. Remember the kid, we got that Glock off of him. The same gun that was used to murder that boy on Bishop Street some months back?" Jones asked, walking up to his partner to bear the good news.

"Yeah, you talking about the kid that's on federal parole, right? What's his name, Marcus?"

"That's him... but check this out. I just got a call from the chief of police in Somerville, Tennessee, saying Marcus's DNA matches DNA left on the scene in a murder of a gun store owner. The individuals also stole massive amounts of guns and ammunition. The owner was found shot in the head. Apparently, one of the culprits vomited on the crime scene and it is that DNA that matches the Marcus kid. So, what this means is, we have proper cause to get an arrest warrant signed by the judge, so we can get his lil muthafucka off the streets," Detective Jones suggested. He despised street niggas and held a personal vendetta with them.

"I agree with you, partner. It's time to take back these streets. These lil gangstas out here starting to think it's sweet and we ain't out there. It's time to start getting our presence felt out here," Detective Flowers responded, supporting his partner.

Flowers and Jones were alike in a lot of ways. Both college graduates, with Detective Jones graduating from Northwestern University and Detective Flowers coming from the University of Illinois. Both participated in sports, specifically football. They were both single and on the dating scene. Through the week they served to protect and get gang gangstas and killas off the street, and the weekend was used to chase sweet young pussy.

"I'm about to head down to the courts to see if I can get his warrants signed by the judge. If everything goes right, we can get the dip shit off the streets tonight," Detective Jones said, putting his firearm in its holster.

"I'm coming with you. Ain't no sense in me just sitting here on my ass. Let's get to it." Detective Flowers left with his partner in hopes to take another violent criminal off the streets of Chicago.

CHAPTER 21

"Yeah, baby. Just like that. You gotta kiss the pussy like you tongue kissing it, boo. That's right, just like that," Stacy purred in ecstasy while Marcus had his dreaded head between Stacy's thick thighs, feasting on her fat twat. After giving Stacy two breathtaking orgasms, Marcus got up and unbuttoned his Rockstar jeans, removing his jeans and boxer briefs.

Marcus's veiny thick penis stood at attention. All ten inches of it. Stacy took his pole inside of her mouth, first she licked around the mushroom and then stuck her tongue inside the pee hole. She jerked him with two hands, while staring him in his eyes, giving him the best head he ever had, sucking his cock from the side then going down to his heavy nut sac.

Marcus was about to explode, but he was having none of that and pulled his dick out of Stacy's mouth. "What, are you scared of this shit, boy?" Stacy said with plenty of lust in her voice, as her pussy was already dripping wet from the way Marcus was just sucking on her pussy.

He laid Stacy on her back and admired her flawless beauty. Stacy was five foot four, thick in all the right places. She was mixed with white and Cambodian, with her Cambodian heritage giving her an exotic look. Stacy was a stripper at a club in Green Bay, Wisconsin called the Cat Box. Marcus had met her at a mall in Chicago about a month ago and had been sexing her ever since.

Marcus leaned down and took one of her dark nipples in his mouth. To Marcus, Stacy had the prettiest set of titties he had ever seen. Her double D's were natural, so were her meaty ass cheeks that made every man she walked past turn their heads to get a glimpse of her donkey ass.

"Put it in, baby. You playing games," Stacy moaned, at the same time, putting her warm tongue in Marcus's ear. Her tongue felt like silk in his ear. Marcus was done with the foreplay and slid his tool in the tight warmness of her love box.

The tightness alone made him want to shoot his load. Marcus started with slow deep strokes that had Stacy going crazy, her manicured nails penetrated the skin on his back. He felt pain and pleasure as he dished it out to Stacy. Seeing that he had her right where he wanted her, he sped up his pace and was now beating the pussy up. The sound of sweaty flesh slapping against each other and the moans of pleasure filled the room.

Ten minutes later, Marcus pulled out of Stacy. Feeling his climax at its peak, Marcus stroked his dick and in three strong spurts, shot his warm nut all over Stacy, coating her stomach, chest, and the bottom of her chin with his semen.

"God damn, girl. That shit so good," Marcus said collapsing on his back, spent from the dick game he had just given Stacy.

"You heard what Beyoncé said, nigga. If you like it then you should of put a ring on it," Stacy said, waving her ring finger in Marcus's face. Marcus chuckled slightly.

"And you heard what Money Bagg Yo said too. Couldn't do nothing with her finger, so I put a ring on her toes," Marcus rapped with a comeback of his own.

He was digging Stacy. There was no question about that, but since his he'd gotten released from federal custody, he made a vow he would never give his heart to a woman again. Not after his baby mama Shawna had left him for dead in the belly of the beast. No family, moral or fictional support. When Shawna sent him an email saying she wasn't going to wait for him for a hundred and twenty months, or ten years, his heart was broken into pieces.

At first, Marcus thought Shawna was acting funny because some young nigga was dicking her down, and she was just going through a phase and would come back once she found out the nigga wasn't shit. Marcus wasn't a deadbeat dad to his daughter Ahvinanna and treated Shawna like a queen, spoiling her with anything his drug money could afford.

So, when Shawna had her phone number changed and blocked his email, he knew that it was a wrap. Days turned to weeks, weeks turned to months, and months to years since he had communicated with his daughter and baby mama. At that moment, Marcus promised himself he would never let a bitch have that much control over his emotions.

Stacy got off the bed, tying her hair in a ponytail.

"Whatever, boy. What are you about to do? I have to go to Walmart real quick," Stacy said, making her way to the bathroom to clean the after-sex off of her.

Marcus grabbed the half a blunt out the ashtray and sparked it. Exhaling the smoke, he said, "I'm about to bounce up outta here. I got some moves to make," as Stacy was coming out of the bathroom with a soapy washcloth to clean Marcus up.

"You are coming back tonight? I was planning on cooking for you tonight." Stacy used the towel to wipe Marcus down.

"We'll see how it go, lil mama," Marcus retorted, taking a pull from the blunt.

Stacy was in the shower when Goon and Capri walked in the bedroom. Capri was Stacy's roommate. She was five-eleven, slim-thick and dark-skinned. Capri was also a stripper at the Cat Box. While Marcus was in the room laying the dick down, Goon was in the next room, breaking Capri's back in.

"You right on time, Scud. A nigga definitely need to make a smoke run," Goon said, reaching for the blunt Marcus was smoking on.

"Don't even trip, we about to bounce anyway. It's time to get in the field. You feel me?"

"Ain't no question," Goon replied, smoking the blunt to the fingertips. He put it out in the ashtray.

"Um, Goon, I gotta work tonight. And you fucked my hair up. Let me get some money so I can get my hair done." Goon looked Capri up and down before he went in the pocket of his Balmain jeans and pulled out a ridiculous knot of cash and peeled off three crispy, blue face hunnids and handed them to Capri.

"Thank you, baby!" she said excitedly and put the bills in her Victoria's Secret bra before she left the room to get ready for her day.

"Aye, my nigga, I was meaning to tell you. You got to stop all that moaning and shit. The hoe got you in here moaning like you the bitch or something. You know their walls thin as shit," Goon said, taking a seat at the head of the California king size bed.

"Man, fuck you. Wasn't nobody moaning, that was her moaning," Marcus solidly defended, pulling up his jeans.

"Man, what the fuck ever, my nigga. I know what I heard. That bitch had you in here curling your toes," Goon said, grabbing a small photo album filled with different pictures of Stacy and her friends at different clubs, having a good time. Looking through the pictures Goon stopped at one particular picture. He saw a picture of Stacy and a young man who was draped in jewelry. They were posing in front of a Dodge Hellcat.

"Ain't no way. Aye, check it out real quick, bruh," Goon said with his gaze fixed on the picture. Marcus pulled his wife beater over his head, walking over to see what Goon was talking about. "This nigga look familiar?" Marcus grabbed the photo album from Goon.

"Look at this pussy ass nigga!" Marcus said, seeing one of his OP's hugged up with his side bitch. Staring back at them was one of his enemies. He was the enforcer for the Get It Boy Clique. In the picture was none other than Choppa.

"What y'all looking at?" Stacy said, coming out the bathroom wrapped in a thick large bath towel. The smell of her fruity Bath and Body Works bath soap graced the airwaves of the bedroom, mixing its smell with marijuana and the smell of after-sex. She caught them looking at a picture of her and Choppa. Choppa was one of her old flames. It started with Choppa being one of her favorite tricks, as Choppa would always come into the club and make it rain.

"Y'all know Choppa?" she asked, peering over Marcus's right shoulder. Marcus was startled by her presence but played it like a player.

"Naw baby, I don't know buddy. We were just looking at his whip, that Hellcat is official. I see he got them Forgiatos on this bitch. See if shorty wanna sell this joint," Marcus said, trying to throw Stacy off.

"I don't think he got that car no more. But I'll ask him for you," Stacy replied suspiciously. Marcus laced up his Giuseppe sneakers and kissed Stacy on the head.

"I think I'mma take you up on your offer for dinner."

"You make sure you do that. Bring your mans with you too," Stacy said, looking over at Goon. "Me and Capri got a surprise for y'all. Compliments of the Cat Box."

Marcus and Goon looked at each other with perplexed looks on their faces. They both knew Stacy and Capri were thots. And the lustful look in Stacy's eyes let them know they were in for a freaky night. Something they both looked forward to.

Marcus and Goon left Stacy's condo to hit the streets. They had to check up on the potential robbery of a mid-level drug dealer that sold bags of Kush on Chicago Avenue and Ridgeway on the city's west side. The block was known to do numbers as high as fifty geez a night. Enough money to leave a nigga's brains leaking in the streets, which they planned to do.

KI walked out of Nieman Marcus with two bags full of clothes. She was on her way to Foot Locker to cop some Nike foam Pockets to go with one of her outfits. She was at Evergreen Plaza spending a few bands. KI was in the streets, getting her weight up. Since going on moves with T.H.C., her bank account had begun to flourish.

After robbing Blue Cheese and his people of their money and jewels, the crew took the hot jewelry down to Virginia where Omega knew somebody that could fence the stolen jewelry. The diamond chains they took off of Blue Cheese and his entourage was estimated to be worth more than five million dollars in cash, which they cashed out for four hundred and fifty grand. Divided between five people, they was able to walk away with ninety stacks a piece, not to mention the sixty in cash they also confiscated from the paper.

With the robberies all together, KI was sitting over three hundred racks of blood money. KI's ambition was fueled by her smart long-term goals, which was to get her money all the way up and buy into a marijuana dispensary. She had a blood cousin that lived in Denver, Colorado, who knew a white boy that was trying to get into the business, all he needed was the financial backing. That's where KI came into play. Her plan was, once she got a half-million, she was going to step away from the crime and murder in Chicago, head to Colorado and go legit.

KI's phone rang inside of her Birkin bag at the same time she walked through the front door of Foot Locker. Looking at the caller ID, she saw that it was Omega calling and answered.

"What's good?" she answered, making her way to where the foam Pockets were.

"Where are you at?"

"Damn, nigga, you questioning me like we fucking or something," KI retorted, looking at a pair of Retro 4 Jordan's on the wall.

"If we were fucking, you wouldn't have that lil funky attitude. You better believe that," Omega said.

"Yeah whatever, Omega. What's up?"

"I need you to come scoop me real quick. I need you to take me on Western so I can get my car out the shop."

"Well, you have to wait until I finish shopping. I'm at Evergreen Plaza, give me about an hour," KI said.

"Alright. And KI?"

"What?"

"Hurry your ass up!" Omega said, ending the call. After trying on a few pair of shoes, KI stood in line to pay for her shoes.

"Hi, ma'am. Will there be anything else?" the cashier asked after ringing up KI's items.

"No, that's it."

"Okay. Your total comes to two-twenty-eight-sixty," the cashier said and started to bag KI item. KI went in her handbag to get her wallet. She handed the cashier three, hundred-dollar bills.

"Thank you," Ki said genuinely, looking up at the familiar face. She could swear she knew him from somewhere. Where, she couldn't put a finger on it.

He was very tall, almost six-one, dark-skinned with long neat dreads down his back. He was dressed in all designer clothes. A black Marc Jella V-neck fitted t-shirt, Givenchy cargo shorts, and Mauri sneakers laced his size eleven and a half feet. KI's attention was captivated by the iced-out Marc Jacobs watch that surrounded his wrist. His facial features gave him a Kevin Garnett appearance, the Versace cologne was doing numbers on KI. She was definitely turned on by the man standing before her.

"Um, excuse me, don't I know you from somewhere?" she questioned.

The man rubbed his thin goatee before he responded, smoothly. "Yeah, you remember me from your dreams. You telling me I ain't been on your mind?" the man said with a smile, showcasing his sparkling grill that was lit up with crushed ice and white gold,

"Boy, please! Like I said, where I know you from?" KI probed, this time with a more serious tone. The man peeped it but was unfazed by her small show of aggression. He was a "street nigga in the streets" nigga, shit. He stayed in character.

"Naw, baby girl, I don't remember you from anywhere. I would've definitely remembered seeing somebody as fine as you," the man said, staring KI in her eyes as he spoke. KI stared back at him, because she couldn't break eye contact with him.

"Check it out, baby girl, what's your name? My name Big Carl. You can call me Carl, though." Big Carl stretched his hand out to shake her hand. KI stared at his hand for a second before she accepted his handshake.

"My name Keisha. Nice to meet you," KI said, shaking his hand softly. She didn't remember where he saw him, but she figured it would come to her. But whoever this Big Carl guy was, made her feel a certain feeling between her thick caramel thighs. Carl moved in for the kill.

"Okay, now that we are friends, why don't you check out my Instagram page, so you can see I ain't one of these lil niggas out here and I'm on some grown man shit." KI smiled at him before she reached in her bag to get her iPhone out.

"Okay, grown man, what's your page info?" Carl gave KI the information she needed to log on to his Instagram page. Scrolling through his page, KI couldn't help but be impressed by Big Carl's street resume. On his Instagram page was nothing but pictures of Big Carl stunting. He drove a white Wraith, a Bentley Ghost and a Rolls Royce Cullinan. She could tell he was papered up. After scrolling through his page, she put her phone back in her bag.

"Okay, then. I see you're out there doing good. That's what's up. So, now what?" KI said, now putting the ball in his court. She wanted him to make the first move. Carl stepped up to KI.

"Shorty, let me get some information. I'm coming to pick you up later. I can take you anywhere you wanna go. Anywhere," Big Carl said with conviction.

"You must got me twisted, baby boy, if you think your Instagram gone get you some pussy. I don't move like that, boo. This is definitely not that," KI informed him, letting him know she wasn't going out like that. She wanted nothing more than for Big Carl to pipe her down. Big Carl smirked before he responded to her comment.

"Baby girl, I can't even lie and tell you I am not attracted to you. You are surely a dime piece and to keep it real with you, if I had you on my arm, niggas would know I got the baddest chick in the city. Straight up!" Big Carl's assertiveness made her smile, which she hadn't done in a while. She had been in the streets putting in work, so her heart was ice cold. That was, until she met the fine specimen of man she was talking to.

"How about this?" Ki said, getting her phone back out the bag. "You give me your number and if my schedule permits, I will give you a call. Maybe we can get a bite to eat or something." KI saved his number and social media contact info. After a few more minutes of conversation and the two of them making plans to see each other, KI left the mall floating on a cloud. Normally, a nigga like Carl would have made The Homicide Crew's most-wanted list, but KI felt something different with Big Carl. What it was she didn't know, but she did know it felt different from the pain, violence and pressure the blood-soaked streets of the Chi produced.

CHAPTER 22

Marcus sat behind the wheel of a Chrysler Town and Country minivan. Goon sat silently in the passenger seat, high off some marijuana they had just smoked. The two of them were on their way to Chicago Avenue and Ridgeway to a weed spot that sold quarter-ounce bags of loud. Marcus drove the minivan down Kedzie Street.

The block they were about to rob was run by a young hustler who went by the name of Jello. Jello was a Conservative Vice Lord, who had an uncle in the feds. His uncle left him with the block, as well as the California plug that sent Jello pounds of weed through the mail every month faithfully.

Goon had met Jello at an after party a few months back and had been copping quarter-ounce bags of weed off Chicago Ave and Ridgeway religiously. Jello had said some slick shit on Facebook, about how he was getting the pounds for the low and busting niggas over the head by overtaxing niggas.

That comment alone was enough to get Goon on his bullshit and put Jello on T.H.C.'s wanted list. The Homicide Crew had their bag all the way up. It wasn't the money that motivated them, but the fear they instilled in the streets of Chi-Raq.

Goon had bought weed on Chicago Avenue and Ridgeway enough times to know the routine security structure of Jello's workers that sold his drugs for him. Goon had done his homework and broke down the structure of the drug crew. At the beginning of the block, two men posted up on security, watching for the police and other potential threats. These two thugs would also direct traffic to the middle of the block, where the dealers would serve them the weed. At the end of the block two more gangsters posted up, playing the same position as the other two thugs on the corner. They were there for security purpose, to protect the land they claimed as their own.

The minivan came to a stop at a red light on Kedzie and Chicago Avenue. It was 10:30 at night and the traffic on the west side streets was mild. Marcus looked over at Goon, who was staring out the window on the passenger side. "So, how do we go about this, my nigga? We both get out to put in the work or what?" Marcus asked, wanting to know how the lick was going to play out.

Goon continued to stare out the window as he laid out the plot.

"Nah bruh, this is how we do it. The nigga with the money bag and the weed gone be in the middle of the block, so you gone have to pull in the alley and park. I'm a get out and creep through the gangway and get the ups on the nigga. Once I do what I do, I'm a come back through the same gangway, hop back in the van and we gone bounce." Goon schooled like it was nothing at all. Goon was named Goon by the streets, because of his addiction to murder and violence. The light turned green and Marcus made a left on Chicago Avenue.

"Man, you sure you don't want me to get out with you? What if something goes wrong? Don't you think two guns are better than one?" Marcus asked, wanting to go without incident.

"My nigga, I already told you they got security in both ends of the block. How well did we pull the move without drawing attention? I got this shit, family. Just stay on point and keep the van running," Goon assured.

Ten minutes later, Marcus pulled the van into a dark alley off of Ridgeway Street. Marcus killed the lights to the vehicle. Goon checked the high capacity magazine to the FNH handgun. Seeing it was loaded to capacity, he stuck the clip back into the weapon and chambered a 5.62 round into the cold chamber. After pulling a black ski mask over his face, Goon pulled his hoodie over his head and tied the drawstrings completely sealing his identity. Looking at his watch, the time read 10:45 pm.

"Give me six minutes, Scud. If I ain't back by then, pull up and see what the bizness is."

"Say less," was Marcus's only reply before he gave Goon some dap. Goon tucked the gun on his waist and got out of the van and into the darkness of the gangway.

Tom Tom sat on the hood of his Buick Lucerne as a thick female stood between his legs, smoking a blunt of Kush. Her name was Temika and she was Tom Tom's baby mama. Tonight was Friday and Temika was waiting for her baby daddy to finish his shift on the block. Tom Tom was Jello's worker who pumped weed for him on Chicago Avenue and Ridgeway. Temika took a pull from the blunt and passed it to Tom Tom.

"Baby, are we still going to be able to hit the liquor store? I need a bottle of Cîroc," Temika asked.

"You just chill, shawty. We gone bounce from over here in about thirty minutes," Tom Tom said, hitting the weed. A black Trailblazer pulled up in front of them and the passenger side window came down.

"Aye fam, let me get three of these quarter bags," the passenger said, holding the money out the window. Tom Tom got off the hood of the car and got in his whip, where he had a Walmart bag full of weed. He got three bags and put the Walmart bag back under the passenger seat. After getting back out, he went to the driver's side of the Trailblazer to serve the customers.

Goon was kneeling down between two houses, laying in the darkness with his gun at his side, watching Tom Tom and the drug activity on Ridgeway intently, waiting patiently to make his move. After watching the Trailblazer turn the corner, Goon knew it was show time and ascended from the gangway, gun extended. Tom Tom was adding the three hundred dollars he'd just made to his massive wad of blue faces, when he heard footsteps rushing behind him. Turning around to see what was going on behind him, he was now face-to-face with Goon's hammer. "Lay it down, pussy nigga. This a robbery. Don't make it no ambulance pick-up." Goon sneered from behind the ski mask.

"Come on, my nigga, that ain't about nothing," Tom pleaded, raising his hands to the sky.

"Uh-uh. Hell naw," Temika cried out, grabbing Goon by the sleeve of his black Nike hoodie, trying to take up for her man. Her heart and bravery in the presence of danger was real nigga shit. But Goon was unfazed by her act of bravery and slapped her across the face with the FN, causing the meat on her forehead to split upon contact. Blood leaked profusely from the wound as she fell to the concrete.

"Let them have it, baby," Tom Tom cried as he saw the mother of his child on the ground leaking. He got on his knees. Goon rushed him, putting the gun to the back of his head.

"Where the weed at, nigga?" Goon growled.

"It's under the passenger seat." Goon looked under the passenger seat of the vehicle and saw the Walmart bag full of weed.

"Run them pockets too, my nigga." Goon searched Tom Tom and relieved him of his day's profit. Goon was about to flee the scene of the crime, until Tom Tom made the grave mistake of sending a threat.

"Bitch ass nigga, we gone find out who you is and trust in believe when we do, it's Desert Storm!" Tom Tom vowed. Goon stepped in his tracks. The Homicide Crew was on a mission to make their presence felt in the drug trade in Chicago. The home of Al Capone.

Goon walked over to Tom Tom and raised his weapon. Tom Tom put his hands over his face as if he could block whatever was about to be released. Goon pulled the trigger and the slight recoil caused the gun to jerk in his right hand. The hot lead penetrated Tom Tom's skull, blowing his brains out in a pinkish mist. He felt nothing as he was sent into complete darkness as death took over his life.

Temika let out a piercing scream that could be heard ten city blocks away. Goon pointed the smoking FN in her direction and was about to squeeze the trigger, when he heard the sirens getting closer and closer. The loud gunshot had awakened the quiet block and now nosy neighbors were looking out their windows and were now sitting first row at the murder show. Goon stared at Temika through the eyes of the devil. He held her life in his hands.

Through clenched teeth, he said, "Tell 'em The Homicide Crew did this." Goon disappeared back into the dark gangway.

"Pull off, my dude," Goon said after getting back in the car. Marcus put the minivan in drive and calmly pulled out of the alley.

"I heard the gunshot. You cool, my nigga?"

"Yeah, I'm good. Nigga wanted to be a gangsta. So, I gave him what he was looking for," Goon replied. Another body added to his body count.

"Where are we about to go now?" Goon asked, pulling off this hoodie that reeked of death.

"We are about to chill at shorty Stacy's crib. I know you ain't forget about the surprise they said they had for us," Marcus said, checking his surroundings in the rearview mirror.

"Oh yeah, I forgot all about that." Goon had forgotten all about the little freak session they had planned. He had just done a murder and some pussy and some good free weed would definitely calm his nerves.

Later that night, Marcus and Goon were at Stacy's condo. The light was dim inside the crib, while Keisha Cole played softly in the background. The smell of Kush and raw sex hung strongly in the air. Marcus laid on his back while Stacy had her head between his legs, giving him head. At the same time, Goon was behind her, giving it to her doggy style. He was pounding at her tight walls like a jack hammer, while Capri watched from the couch playing with her swollen clit.

When Marcus and Goon returned from the robbery they were shocked to come into the condo to find Stacy and Capri in thongs and bras. A porno played on the seventy-five-inch smart television. After a few blunts of loud and a fifth of Grey Goose, everybody was in a lustful bliss.

"Ahhh shit," Goon groaned, before he pulled out of Stacy and shot his sperm all over her back and ass cheeks. A few moments later, Marcus was spilling his seeds down Stacy's throat, causing her to gag. Once the extreme sex session was over, the four of them sat up smoking blunts and chilling.

"Man, Joe. We ain't got no more blunts?" Goon asked, seeing they had rolled the last Backwood and had an empty box.

"It's some in the glove compartment in the van," Marcus let him know, while Stacy ran her manicured nails across his tattooed chest. Goon didn't want to be the one to go get the blunts, but he wanted to smoke. Throwing his jeans on and a T-shirt, he left out to go get the blunts.

Two minutes later, after Goon went to get the blunts, Marcus's cell phone vibrated on the table in front of him. Grabbing it, he looked at the caller ID and saw it was Goon calling. "What the fuck!" He thought of himself before he answered. He called.

"Yo!"

"Aye, my nigga, came out the crib now! It's a car parked on the side of these bitches' crib. It looks like some niggas in the whip. My gun in my jacket up there where you at. Come outside, my nigga." Marcus's heart started to beat fast as he jumped up and slid on his jeans.

"What's wrong, baby?" Stacy asked, seeing how Marcus was moving. He ignored her question and continued to put on his clothes. After putting on his jacket, Marcus grabbed Goon's Pelle Pelle jacket and got the FN and rushed out the crib.

Once Marcus walked out the house, he noticed a black Porsche truck with tinted windows, parked on the side of Stacy's condo. But no signs of Goon. Marcus walked swiftly to the van with the FN at his side. Ready for action, jumping in the driver's seat, it was like everything went in slow motion. The loud gunshot cracked, breaking the silence as a bullet whizzed past his dome, shattering the driver's side window. The sound of the thunderous gunshot made Marcus get active.

Pointing his firearm out the window toward the gunshots, Marcus squeezed the trigger and let the FNH speak. Rapid shots lit up the night as the door to the Porsche truck flung open and a man hopped out, letting loose in an attempt to shoot and kill Marcus. With no other choice but to flee, as he was outgunned, Marcus frantically put the key in the ignition and brought the engine to life. At the same time, bullets penetrated the van from the hellacious gunfire, Marcus pulled off just as a bullet shattered the back window. With his blood pressure up and his adrenaline pumping, he reached in his jacket and got his cell phone to call Goon's phone. The call went straight to voicemail.

"Fuck. Where you at, my nigga?" Marcus said out loud. He was worried about Goon's well-being. He didn't know where Goon was. Nor did he know who was just trying to end his life, but he had a strong feeling Stacy and Capri had something to do with it. How else did the niggas know where he was at? He vowed that if he found out they had something to do with the situation, he was going to crush them. Period.

The Homicide Crew was starting to make a lot of enemies in the streets, it could've been anybody that was at their head. They was in the streets robbing and killing niggas. Chicago was crazy. At any moment, the predator could easily become the prey.

CHAPTER 23

BACK IN LEWISBURG

It had been two days since YaYo had hollered at Lil G about this paperwork. The whole weekend, YaYo and Nino waited patiently for Lil G to call down there to try and fish his work for them, to no avail. Now they were about to go to the recreation cage. Dread, who was a Black Soul from the west side of the city had presented his legal documents and came back an official nigga that had received a life sentence for distribution of heroin. He took his sentence like a G.

"So, what's the demonstration once we get you in this rec cage, my nigga?" Nino asked YaYo as he made his bunk, so when the CO came to get them for recreation, their cell would be in compliance. So, they wouldn't get banged from rec.

"You already know, family. If he ain't got that paperwork with him in that cage when we get down there, he gotta hit that gate. Just as simple as that. He can go by choice or he can go by force and get crushed," YaYo replied.

"So, you willing to get set back to day-one phase one, all over a nothing ass nigga?" Nino had been trying to talk YaYo out of prison politics. Trying to get him to see the logic that getting out the S.M.U. was more important than trying to prove a point. YaYo was hearing none of that and made his mind up to stand on morals and principle. YaYo was getting frustrated with Nino's analogy on the situation.

"I already told you, Nino, what the business is with this nigga and that's what I'm standing on. And no disrespect to you, my nigga, but I'm getting tired of going back and forth with you about the business. You don't have to roll with this demonstration. Hell, you don't even have to go down to the rec cage. I got this, nigga," YaYo assured Nino as he heard the correctional officers coming down the tier to take the inmates to rec.

Nino just shook his head, he knew YaYo had made up his mind and there was nothing he could do or say to talk the young gangster out of what he was about to do.

Two C.O.'s came and stepped in front of YaYo's cell. Cell

"How many for recreation?" the tall white officer asked, peering into YaYo's cell, trying to find something out of place so he could bang them for recreation. He found nothing. YaYo raised two of his fingers to indicate that both he and his celly would be signing up for rec. The C.O. wrote YaYo and Nino's names down on a clipboard, then used his keys to unlock the food slot.

Once the food slot was opened, YaYo bent down and stuck his hands out the slot, allowing the officer to slap cold handcuffs around his wrists. After YaYo was handcuffed, he stood up and stepped to the side to allow Nino to get cuffed up. After both inmates were secured in handcuffs, the C.O. grabbed his walkie talkie and spoke into it.

"This is D-Block Range 3. Pop cell number 16." Seconds later, YaYo's cell door popped open. YaYo walked backward toward the C.O. that grabbed him by the chain of his handcuffs and escorted him to the recreation cage. YaYo walked out of D-Block and the hot sun shined down upon him, causing him to squint his eyes. The weather was hot and humid as the heat index in Pennsylvania reached over a hundred degrees and it was only 9:00 in the morning.

The C.O. walked YaYo to recreation cage number 7 and stopped. Nino and his escorting officer were standing behind them. YaYo looked in the cage and saw Lil G standing in the corner of the cage with a mean mug on his face. He also noticed Dread wasn't in the cage. Uncuffed, YaYo waited until the two C.O.'s walked off and bent the corner of the walkway.

"What good, fam, you got that work?" YaYo asked, getting right to it. He didn't have time for frivolous conversation. Lil G got off the cage, now on point.

"YaYo, my nigga. I already told you I'm official. Call the streets on me," Lil G said.

"And like I already told you, nigga, we ain't doing the vouching thing. I don't give a fuck who know you, my nigga. We need to see that work, and if you ain't trying to present it, then you need to get out the cage with us, because we all got our work in this bitch," YaYo said through clenched teeth.

Lil G matched YaYo's aggression as he responded, "My nigga, you putting all that bass in your voice like you intimidating a nigga. Nigga, I'm with the shit too." YaYo was tired of the fake thug that stood before him popping slick with all the gangster shit. YaYo and Nino already knew Lil G was hot. The third shift C.O. had already looked him up for YaYo and Nino. The conclusion was that Lil G had snitched about a body. Lil G was about to say some more slick shit until YaYo snuck him, landing a strong, calculated punch on Lil G's chin, causing him to stumble backwards into the corner of the rec cage. YaYo rushed him, landing blow upon blow to Lil G's face and torso. Lil G could do nothing but ball up and try to protect his head and face from the blows YaYo was dishing out.

"Now hit that gate, you bitch ass nigga!" YaYo said, almost out of breath from the work he had just put in, his knuckles scarred and bloody from the assault.

Lil G was dizzy as he tried to make his way to the front of the cage, leaking, face swollen, and plenty of knots on his head.

Nino, not wanting to be left out on the work and to show his loyalty to his brother, punched Lil G in the jaw breaking it. The punch sent Lil G to the concrete where he laid in his own blood, until the C.O.'s did their fifteen-minute rounds and noticed him on his back, needing plenty of medical attention.

"Man down. I repeat, man down," the C.O. yelled into his walkie talkie. Seconds later, a bunch of C.O.'s with riot gear and gas guns flooded the front of cage number 7. YaYo and Nino were doing burpees as if they had nothing to do at the bloody assault.

"You do another damn burpee, I swear to God," one of the correctional officers yelled and stuck the barrel of his gas gun through the cage, with his sweaty finger on the trigger ready to squeeze. YaYo and Nino laid on the hot concrete with their hands on top of their heads. A stretcher was brought to the rec cage and Lil G was loaded on it and rushed to medical.

After Lil G was out of the recreation cage, the C.O. handcuffed YaYo and Nino behind their backs and escorted them back inside of D-Block. Once inside the holding cell, YaYo and Nino were told to strip naked as the day they were born.

An officer with a small digital camera took pictures of YaYo's swollen, bloody knuckles. "So, you must be the one that was putting in all the work. You were punching that inmate like you were Mike Tyson. What the hell did he do to you?" the officer asked, fishing for information about the fight. YaYo remained silent.

"Yeah, whatever, tough guy." The C.O. slid YaYo back his clothing and told him to get dressed. After the two convicts was searched, they were led back to their cell on D-Block. A lot of inmates looked out the small window in their cells, seeing the two gangsters standing in front of the cell waiting to get let in. A lot of them gave head nods as a show of respect. They knew they had just shed blood inside the recreation cage.

"Pop cell 16," the C.O. spoke into the walkie talkie. Once in the small cell and their handcuffs taken off, the correctional officer closed the food slot and locked it.

You good, fam?" Nino asked YaYo as he watched him run cold water over his hands.

"Yeah, I'm good, Ock. Fucked around and punched that damn fence. Plus, that nigga had a hard ass head," YaYo replied with a slight chuckle.

"I'm already hip, my dude," Nino said, taking off his bloody thermal top.

After the men cleaned themselves up, they sat on their bunks conversating when a man they had never seen at the prison before, came to the cell door.

"Anderson, Lawrence, come to the door." YaYo hopped off his bunk and went to the cell door, Nino stood behind him. The man had some papers in his hand.

"My name is Agent Thomas, FBI. I just want the both of you to know your disciplinary shot will be forwarded to the feds to be processed. If they see fit, then you both will be indicted for the assault. If not, it'll be kicked back to administration here at Lewisburg where it will be sent to DHO, the Disciplinary Hearing Officer," Agent Thomas informed them and slid two pieces of paper under the cell door. YaYo picked them up. "Be looking to have something back from the feds in about a week. You will be reached by mail. Good luck, fellas," was all Agent Thomas said before he walked off.

"Ain't no way they about to try and give us some more time for that bullshit. I done put niggas on Med-Flights and didn't get cased up. Now they trying to indict me for a fucking fist fight?" YaYo said in frustration, not believing what he was going through.

"YaYo, this the S.M.U. All shots get sent to the feds to get processed, it's just a procedure, don't trip. They'll kick it back, it's just a minor assault. What that shit say anyway?" Nino inquired. YaYo read the disciplinary shit out loud.

"It says, On June 16, 2018, while monitoring Nice Vision, video footage of a non-witnessed assault in the east side of recreation cage number 7 the following was discovered. At approximately 9:17 a.m. on the video screen, Inmate Anderson, Yaton 07505-424 is seen striking Inmate Watts, Cidney 46902-424 in the facial area with closed fist punches.

At the time, Inmate Watts goes to the corner of the recreation cage. At approximately 9:18 a.m. on the video screen, Inmate Lawrence, Tony 21770-424 joins the altercation and begins to strike Inmate Watts in the face with a closed fist punch. Inmates Anderson and Lawrence then ceased their actions and separated until staff responded to the recreation cage to remove all inmates."

YaYo finished reading the 224 assault shot, then gave Nino his copy, before he climbed back in the top bunk. Nino glanced over the shot.

"YaYo, I wouldn't worry too much about this as for getting more time, but we definitely are going to get set back day-one, phase one. But you already knew that was going to happen."

"I ain't tripping, Ock, sometimes it's all about the brand, we can't let nothing tarnish that," YaYo said, letting Nino know he would always stand on principle and on his beliefs, no matter the consequences.

"I feel you, fam. At least you stand on your word. I respect that and that's a beautiful characteristic to have." Nino gave YaYo his respects. He liked how YaYo went into goon mode and took off on Lil G in the cage.

A WEEK LATER

It was 4:30 in the afternoon inside Lewisburg Penitentiary. The best part of the day, mail call. YaYo and Nino was in the cell chilling. YaYo was in his bunk, reading a book on limited liability companies while Nino rested, taking a quick power nap. The C.O. walked on the tier passing out mail, stopping in front of YaYo's cell and slid two pieces of mail under the door. YaYo got off the bunk and grabbed the mail.

After unfolding the paper that had his name on it, YaYo saw it was the decision on his shot, to see if the feds was going to indict him for the assault in the recreation cage. Reading, YaYo started to smile. Not only did the FBI kick the shot back, they dropped the shot all together, because the office who wrote the shot up, used the wrong date on the shot, making the shot bogus.

There would be no disciplinary sanctions, so there would be no day-one, phase one. YaYo and Nino had just received a blessing. They had layed down a demonstration in Lewisburg to let niggas and the administration know what they would stand for and what they wasn't going to stand for. "Aye Nino, check it out, fam. The feds kicked our shit back, and they dropped the shot!" YaYo was ecstatic, waking Nino from his nap. Nino slowly awakened.

"Oh yeah? Let me see that." YaYo passed Nino the mail. Reading it, Nino started to smile. Nino was surely glad he didn't have to start the program over. Getting more time, he cared nothing about, he was serving a life sentence. He just wanted out of the S.M.U. Nino stood up, facing YaYo.

"Now listen, brother. Allah has just given us a blessing. We laid our lick down, so now these crackers know now not to put no hot niggas in our rec cage. Just sit back and do this last six months and get to the compound," Nino said. He was motivated now that he knew he had a chance of getting out the S.M.U.

"I'm with that, Ock, it's time to bounce up outta here, that six months gone fly by," YaYo said now seeing the bigger picture. He only had a couple years left to serve on his sentence. Then he would be released back to the community. Back to his freedom, his family, and a personal lifestyle.

He would leave the pain and misery in the cold walls of the penitentiary and vow to never return. By all means necessary. YaYo continued. "Yeah Nino, we have another chance, let's just complete their program and get up out of here."

YaYo and Nino continued to do their time in Lewisburg Penitentiary, but YaYo was getting short. He was about to be released. Released to the city of Chicago, his home, in hopes to make a positive change in the streets that he had been birthed from.

CHAPTER 24

"You think this lil gangster is going to go peacefully or are we gone have to fill his ass up with these hollows and then bring him to the station?" Detective Flowers asked his partner as he sat behind the dark tint of the Crown Victoria. A chrome .357 Magnum rested on his lap and he was itching to let it blow. Detective Flowers and Detective Jones were doing surveillance on a house on 34th and Prairie Street. They had a search warrant for the house they were watching.

They had been lamping on the crib for the last couple of days, their intended target, Marcus, had come to the residence last night and had not left the house, so they knew he was still in the residence. Detective Jones sat in the passenger seat of the Crown Vic, looking at the color photo of Marcus. In his other hand, he held the murder warrant.

"His ass better go peacefully or else it is what it is. These lil motherfuckas wanna run around selling dope and killing, that shit gotta stop," Detective Jones said, still looking at Marcus's photo. The plan they were about to execute was simple. They had a no-knock warrant. The entire block of Prairie Street was blocked off, with two unmarked cruisers at the front of the block, two cruisers in the back and a cruiser in the alley behind Marcus's house, just in case he had my bright ideas.

Detective Jones looked at his watch, they had exactly five minutes before they executed the search warrant. After Jones folded up the photo and warrant, he stuck them in his vest pocket. He then grabbed his service Glock from its holster, ejected the magazine to make sure it was full with twenty .40 caliber rounds. After expecting the ammunition, he stuck the magazine back into the butt of the weapon and pulled the slide back, chambering a round. And patiently, he waited.

Marcus sat on the couch inside his lil side chick's house. He had been a nervous wreck, chain smoking cigarette after cigarette. His nerves had been shot ever since the attempt on his life. Marcus had continuously tried to dissect and analyze the recent event but couldn't put the pieces to the puzzle together. Shit wasn't making sense to him at this point.

At first, he tried to reason that Stacy and her roommate had something to do with it, but he had done nothing but show her love, so he quickly dismissed the thought. Then, he thought about the situation with Rockett and how he and Ace had brought Rockett a move. But, the G.B.C. had no idea The Homicide Crew had anything to do with Rockett's murder. Marcus was running out of options, but one thing was for sure, somebody just tried to nail him to the cross. Then, Goon was MIA. Something wasn't making sense. Goon was nowhere to be found and wasn't answering his phone. Shit wasn't adding up.

Marcus picked up the phone and called Ace. He answered.

"What's good, Killa? You heard from Goon yet?" Marcus probed as soon as Ace answered his phone.

"Hell naw, fam, his phone going straight to voicemail still," Ace replied.

"Man, this shit crazy as hell. Niggas shooting at us and shit, and the nigga just fell off the face of the earth," Marcus vented on the phone.

"Aye yo, I hollered at KI yesterday. She said she wanted to get up with us in the am, so we can talk face-to-face about shit. You already know we don't talk or discuss work on the phone. But peep, keep your ear to the streets and stay on point. We gone get to the bottom of all this shit. Trust me."

"Alright that's a bet. Where we meeting up in the morning and what time?" Marcus asked.

"Meet us at the restaurant called E&M Steak and Eggs on 120th and Halsted Street. At 9:30 a.m."

"Alright, bruh," was Marcus's only reply before he ended the call and tossed his phone on the couch. "Fuck!" he cursed to himself out of frustration. He was nervous and had no clue what was going on, or who was trying to put an end to his life.

"Boy, who you got out there shooting at you and shit?" Sweets asked, coming into the living room smoking a blunt. She had overheard Marcus speaking on the phone. Sweets was definitely a nosy bitch. Marcus was about to respond, until the front door was knocked off the hinges.

"Chicago Police! Get on the ground now. Get on the ground now!" Flashlights and Glocks were pointed at the occupants of the house. Marcus put his hands up, scared to death. Sweets laid down, complying with officers.

"Get on the ground, I'm not going to tell you again. Get on the ground," Detective Jones said with aggression. Marcus complied not wanting to get shot. His heart was beating fast. He knew the plainclothes officers were the law when he saw Detective Jones and Detective Flowers. He couldn't believe the cops had put him in the trick bag. He now understood the phrase, "Don't nothing beat the cross but the double cross."

It was 3:30 in the afternoon when Choppa walked through the food court at Ford City Mall. He was there to meet up with his lil thot, Stacy. Choppa and Stacy had been fucking around since Choppa met her at the Cat Box strip club in Wisconsin. He would frequent the spot whenever he wasn't tied up in the streets standing on Nation business, which was a full-time job. Choppa had been in the streets, putting in work in retaliation of his dead homie, Rockett.

He was still looking for Ace or any other of his Homicide Crew affiliates to put bullets in their heads. Choppa would not stop until Ace was buried six feet deep. He had caught up with Marcus and Goon a few nights ago, aimed at their heads and missed. Choppa was frustrated that he had Marcus life in his hands and failed. He got the drop on his OP's from the information Stacy had given him.

Choppa and Stacy had been beefing lately and once Stacy found out Choppa was beefing with The Homicide Crew, Stacy used Marcus as a sacrifice lamb to get back in good graces with Choppa. So, Stacy came up with the diabolical plan to set Marcus up. Marcus was cool and his dick game was proper, but it was Choppa who had the money. And his name was ringing bells in the streets.

Choppa walked through the food court of the mall and spotted Stacy sitting at the table by herself by McDonald's. As he walked to the other table, Stacy let a smile come across her lips, watching Choppa approach her table. She admired his swag, letting her eyes roam over him from head to toe. He was dressed in a fitted Balenciaga sweat suit with Balenciaga written all over it. His dreadlocks hung wild to his shoulders and a G.B.C. charm sprayed in ice hung from a forty-inch Cuban link chain. The diamond studded Cartier frames covered his bloodshot eyes from the blunt of Moon Rock he had just smoked.

"What's good, lil mama? How are you?" Choppa greeted her.

"Waiting on your slow ass. Why do you always have me waiting? Why you can't never be on time?" Stacy fumed with a minor attitude. She had been waiting on Choppa for over an hour. Choppa ignored his interrogation.

"Come on, shorty, I'm trying to put something in my stomach. Let's go to TGI Friday's. We can holler in there."

Choppa and Stacy walked inside TGI Friday's and were seated by the waitress. Choppa ordered a pitcher of Corona beer and two shots of Patrón.

"Will you be ordering now, or should I give you some time?" the waitress asked.

"You can give us a few minutes."

"Okay, that's fine, sir. I will be right back with your drinks. The waitress added with a smile. Choppa and Stacy picked up their menus.

"So, what's up? You said you wanna holler at me, what's on your mind?" Choppa asked, getting right to the point. Stacy texted him, telling him she had some valuable information on some of his opposition, and he was ready to bleed her for all of it. Stacy looked over the top of the menu at him.

"Damn, Choppa! You can't at least ask me how I've been doing or nothing?"

"How are you doing? Now, what's up with them hoe ass niggas?" Choppa said in a tone that let Stacy know he wasn't about the games. And was on business. She put her menu down.

"Well, as you know, I can't stay at the condo no more. Choppa, I'm scared. What if Marcus finds out I set that shit up? I'm not trying to get kilt fucking with you." Choppa went into the front pocket of his joggers and pulled out a thick wad of cash and set it in front of Stacy.

"Bitch, you the one called me with this shit. Fuck is you talking about? That's thirteen stacks to go get another crib. So, what's up?" Stacy took the money and thumbed through the hunnids and fifties, before she put the money in her designer handbag. Stacy proceeded to give Choppa the rundown on the info she had on The Homicide Crew.

"I got a friend named China. She told me she be fucking with a nigga named Omega and that he part of some gang that be robbing drug dealers in the city. He be fucking with Marcus and Goon too. And some nigga named Ace." Choppa listened attentively while Stacy talked about his OP's.

"And?" Choppa probed.

"Well, baby, she know where that nigga lay his head at. I can get the address for you." Choppa looked at her like she was crazy. But in the same mind frame, Stacy was showing him signs of loyalty. So, Choppa took a chance.

"Let me get that info." Stacy gave him all the information she knew about The Homicide Crew. Choppa gave her some lightweight conversation, promising her the house on the beach before he bounced. He went to go grab his hammers, because somebody was definitely about to die.

CHAPTER 25

Today, Quavon had to go to federal court for an initial appearance hearing. Quavon was called to the courtroom and indicted on two federal money laundering charges, for getting caught with three point two million in cash. The U.S. District Attorney provided the government with substantial physical evidence to proceed with trial.

Quavon didn't have a criminal record. His points were low, as the feds went by a point system when sentencing. He would go to the feds at the most fifty-eight months. The government set another court date for October 3 two months away. Quavon walked out of the courthouse with his paid lawyer, C.J. Wisenberg.

"So, like I said, Mr. Anderson, they are offering you three years of supervision if you plead guilty, and if you go to trial, your guide-lines are between thirty-two to fifty-eight months in federal prison," the lawyer said, giving Quavon his options. Quavon wasn't trippin about the supervision. He would rather be on the streets than prison for any time. He was in his feelings more about the money he lost.

"Alright, C.J., I'll plead out to the supervision. I'm not trying to fight these people, they got me red-handed. I can't believe the feds went through all of this. You know, with the bitch Bella," Quavon said, mad at himself for getting played by Bella and Bank Roll Buddy. But it didn't make sense, just for some money? He was confused, but he was going to cop to the supervision.

"I'll keep you posted and notify you of any changes and if you have any questions, don't hesitate to give me a call," Wisenberg said, shaking Quavon's hand.

"Alright, C.J. Just make sure you keep me posted. I pay you a lot of paper, so make sure I get my money's worth," Quavon said and walked off.

Quavon walked over to the parking ramp and got in his Lexus ES300 and pulled out of the lot. The federal case he caught was nothing. That was the least of his problems, he still owed Castilino for a shipment of heroin. The G.B.C. had a lot of money tied up in the stress and the money was coming back slowly. Too slow for Quavon's taste. It was as if the workers were starting to buck, so he ordered Choppa to step his press game up in the streets on collecting tips. Quavon grabbed his phone and placed a call. The phone rang twice before Crusha answered.

"Speak on it, brother."

"C, what's good, bruh? I just left the courthouse."

"Oh yeah? What are they talking about?"

"They gave me another court date, the district attorney talking about three years of supervised probation. But, check it out. I need you to get up with the team and tell them we need to have a mandatory meeting tomorrow at 1:00 pm. We gone meet at Dave and Buster's up north."

Alright, brother, I will give everybody the memo," Crusha replied.

"I appreciate that, big homie. See y'all tomorrow."

"Peace." Quavon ended the call. A lot was going on in the streets. He lost a few mil, caught a fed case and his man Rockett was laid up in a casket. Once Quavon secured the plug and paid Castilino and his men, he was going to restore order back in the streets. While getting money and going through trials and tribulations, the streets had started to think The Get It Boy Clique was out of the way and niggas was trying to test they temperature by putting hands on Rockett.

YaYo had told Quavon years ago that in order to get money and stay in a position of power in the Chi, you had to put in the work, as the murder game and the dope game coincided. YaYo's words of wisdom had not failed him yet.

Ace rode shotgun in the Lincoln MKZ. Behind the wheel was a dope fiend named Alvin. Ace would use Alvin to drive him around his drug blocks to drop off products and pick up cash. Ace knew he had to keep the pole on him, so since Alvin had his driver's license, he gave Alvin a job as his personal driver and paid him in dope. "Pull up to Lawrence Fishery. I'm hungry as shit," Ace told him. They had been in traffic all day grinding and Ace hadn't eaten anything. He was running off of Kush and Percocets.

Ace was feeling himself since they had shot and killed Rockett. The six bricks of heroin they robbed him for was broken down bag for bag and put on the block. The Homicide Crew was eating off the work. The fear that T.H.C. was gaining in the streets seemed to only fuel Ace's ambition. Ace grabbed his iPhone and logged onto Facebook and went live.

"Yeah, niggas... it's Ace, aka Homicide Ace. I just thought I'd show you niggas my face and let you hoe ass niggas see the faces of death. You niggas got it. We coming to get it, Homicide Crew. You bitch niggas, it's homicide and if niggas want smoke, pull up. I'm at Lawrence Fishery right now, come see me." Ace sneered at the camera of his phone, putting on for his team.

Choppa was driving down 25th and State when his phone beeped. Looking at the phone screen, he saw it was a Facebook notification from Ace. Choppa had befriended Ace, using a bogus Facebook account. Choppa couldn't believe his luck, he was only a few blocks away from the restaurant. Choppa's heart started to beat fast as he was getting excited, he smashed the gas, running a stop light to get to Ace.

Three minutes later, Choppa was swerving into the parking lot of Lawrence Fishery and parked on the side of a F-150 pick-up truck. It was 1:30 in the morning. The restaurant closed at 2:00 am, so it was packed with people waiting to get their orders. Choppa reached under the seat and got the Glock .19, focusing his attention towards the entrance of the establishment and waited. Ace had just signed off of Facebook Live only a few minutes ago, which meant he was still in there.

Ace paid for his fried shrimp and fish 'n chips and made his way out of the crowded restaurant. Leaving out, he bumped into a female named Nikia. He had met her on the north side. They fucked a few times and that was that. Seeing how her jeans were hugging her thick frame made him remember how good her pussy was. Ace wanted to tap that ass. He got her number and said he was going to get up with her a lil later. Securing his booty call for the night, Ace made his way to his whip where Alvin was waiting for him.

Choppa watched Ace walk out of the restaurant and looked around the parking lot to see if there were any potential witnesses to what he was about to do. Seeing one, Choppa tilted his White Sox snapback over his eyes and slid his hands in a pair of latex gloves and got out his vehicle. Ace was walking toward his car when somebody said his name.

"Ace, what's good, fam?" Choppa raised the Glock pointing it at Ace's face. Ace dropped his bag of food. It was hard to see the face of the shadow figure that was pointing a gun at him. Ace thought about reaching for the Sig Sauer on his waist. Choppa tightened his finger on the trigger.

"Bitch ass nigga. Nigga tried to fuck with you hoe ass niggas on some work so y'all can eat, but niggas is snakes and maggots. Y'all put hands on the wrong nigga, Rockett was G.B.C. He one of ours." Ace was thoroughbred and wasn't going out like a hoe. He bucked and went for the Sig on his waist, but Choppa peeped the move and squeezed the trigger in rapid succession. The first two slugs caught Ace in the head, blowing his brains out his hat rack, the other two caught his chin and jaw. His body hit the pavement.

Not even waiting to see the body drop, Choppa jogged back to his car, got in and pulled out of the parking lot. Dopefiend Alvin heard the gunshots and he knew it had something to do with Ace. He saw Ace walking to the car and then the gunman approached him, said something and then shot Ace in the face. Seeing the coast was clear, Alvin got out the car and ran over to Ace, who was laying in a puddle of his own blood. Alvin didn't know what to do, except call 911.

WGN NEWS AT 9

"I'm Vanessa Johnson."

"And I'm Tom Holbert and you are tuned in to WGN News at 9. On today's top story, a man was killed in the parking lot of a restaurant on 22nd and Canal Street on the city's south side early this morning. Authorities say Aaron Washington was shot and killed in the parking lot of Lawrence Fishery. Witnesses called police to report sounds of gunshots and when police arrived, they found Aaron Washington unresponsive, with gunshot wounds to the head. Police would like anyone with information to call 911. The homicide is the city's 150th homicide this year…" The news showed Ace's picture on the screen.

"Ahhhhhh!" Omega yelled and threw the bottle of 1800 Tequila he was drinking at his sixty-five-inch Vizio. The screen shattered. The news had just shown Ace's face. Omega couldn't believe his lil potna was dead. He was watching the WGN news by coincidence when the news aired Ace's homicide. Ace was his right-hand man. They had grown up together. It was Ace that came up with the idea to start The Homicide Crew. The tears rolled down Omega's cheek from his heart being broken as he sat, remembering how The Homicide Crew came about.

Omega and Ace were at a trap house on 59th and Bishop Street, cooking and bagging up crack cocaine. Ace sat at the kitchen table in front of a plate, with a razor blade and sandwich bags bagging up 63 grams of crack cocaine, while Omega stood over the stove, watching the cocaine bubble inside the Pyrex. It was 7:30 at night and they was trying to finish doing what they was doing, so they could hit the block and grind.

"Man, I'm tired of all the slow rolling shit. Niggas been hustling forever and we can't een cop over four and a half ounces, it's like we hustling backwards," Ace said, slicing a piece of crack with the razor, while Omega took the Pyrex off the stove and took it to the sink and let cold water run in the Pyrex, hardening the cocaine. After the coke started to get hard, Omega took a fork and start mixing the drug. This was called whipping.

"So, what are you gonna do about it?" Omega asked Ace as he continued to whip the work.

"What do you mean, what am I gonna do about it? I'm a start taking shit from these hoe ass niggas. I'm tired of struggling. Niggas around the city riding around in Wraiths and shit. Soft ass, pussy ass niggas that can't even protect they bread," Ace vented.

"We been out here taking shit. That ain't nothing new," Omega said.

"Naw, fam, we been out here faking. How we out here putting in all this work and a nigga still on the block. I'm a tell you, fam,

because we out here robbing niggas that's struggling like us. I'm talking about hitting rappers, ball players and the brick man. I don't give a fuck. I'm talking about robbing the whole city."

"We gone need a team for that, my nigga," Omega retorted, dumping the rest of the crack on a plate.

"We already got a team. Goon, KI, Marcus. I know they gone be with the shit," Ace said.

Goon was from the Jeffery Manor Projects on the east side, but his family lived on 59th and Bishop, so he was cool with Ace and Omega. Goon was a stick-up kid that didn't mind letting his gun bust. KI lived on 59th and was a thug. She was pretty and thick but dangerous, as she was a hustla that stayed scheming. Marcus was also from 59th and had just come home from a federal bid for a gun. Marcus was gang.

"Well, holler at the guys. I'm with whatever, my nigga, as long as it's conducive to the bank roll," Omega said. After he finished cooking and bagging up crack, Ace got on his cell to call the crew to meet on 59th. After relaying his vision to his people, he wasn't shocked to see everybody was on the same page and wanted the same, to come up. That night, The Homicide Crew was born.

That was a few years and plenty of murders ago. Omega felt as if his life was knocked out of him. His vision was a blur as he didn't know what to do, but somebody had to die for killing Ace. That he was adamant about.

Choppa sat inside his whip parked on the block of 69th and Walcott. He was watching the workers on the block to make sure they were doing what they were supposed to be doing, getting money. What the Get It Boy Clique was all about. Choppa had just crushed Ace, so his morale was all the way up. The Homicide Crew had killed his potna, Rockett. Ace was just the beginning. Choppa wasn't going to stop the killing until everybody that was a part of, or in alliance with The Homicide Crew was dead.

Choppa lit the tip of the blunt he had in his hand. Taking a strong pull from the exotic, he held the smoke in his lungs. As for the murder game in Chi-Raq, Choppa was the self-appointed king. And he was willing to show anyone who said different. He was the enforcer for the G.B.C., the dons of the city and Quavon was willing to take lives to keep his family in that position. And to stand on his blind loyalty, Choppa was going to keep niggas in fear of the Get It Boy Clique.

Ki was sprawled out in the king size canopy bed. Big Carl laid naked next to her sleeping. The two of them were at the Crown Plaza Hotel in Madison, Wisconsin. Ever since their first day, it had been a wrap. KI was digging Big Carl in a major way. And Big Carl was feeling her as well. It had been two weeks since they met and they were inseparable. Big Carl did nothing but spoil KI with designer clothes and wine and dined her at the most exclusive restaurants. Big Carl had also taken KI to Los Vegas to trick off some bands, not to mention, he kept her with a sore pussy and aching back from his superior sex game.

For KI, it wasn't the clothes she was attracted to, but his swag and intellect. She was a boss bitch and her murder game was official, she was a part of a criminal gang in the city that was gaining major influence and attention for their notoriety in the streets. But Big Carl had her mind gone. The more time she spent with Big Carl, the more she started to neglect the streets. KI slid off the bed, grabbed her Dereon handbag and made her way to the bathroom.

Sitting on the toilet, "Shit," KI cursed, rubbing her fingers over her swollen pussy lips as she thought about the events of last night and how Big Carl was ramming his dick in and out of her tight walls. While sitting on the toilet, KI went in her purse and got her iPhone. Looking at the screen, she saw she had seventeen missed calls and ten text messages, all from Omega.

"What the fuck is he sweating my phone like this for?" The last time she saw Omega was two weeks ago, when she picked him up to go get his car. To KI, Omega was starting to act weird when he was around. His questioning of her personal business was starting to irritate her.

They were at a stoplight once, while KI was behind the wheel of her Cadillac Escalade, when a Jag truck pulled up to the light beside her. Omega was in the passenger seat rolling a blunt. The driver of the Jag truck rolled his window down and honked his horn to get KI's attention, he was trying to get her number in traffic. The light turned green and KI pulled off, but not before blowing the driver a kiss.

"What the fuck you all in that nigga face for?" Omega interrogated through clenched teeth from the passenger seat. KI looked at him like he was crazy, before she replied, "Nigga, please." That's when KI knew Omega was losing his mind.

Ki read the text message Omega sent her. Reading it, her jaws dropped to the floor. "Ain't no fucking way!" She continued to read the text. A tear escaped and rolled off her face and landed on her thigh. Her heart stopped a second as she logged on the WGN news app on her phone and read the segment on Ace's homicide. She couldn't believe Ace was dead. Ace was like her little brother, she had mad love for him. She began to cry uncontrollably.

Dropping her phone on the floor, KI stood up and walked over to the shower and turned it on. She was in a daze from what she'd just found out. Once the water was hot, she stepped into the shower and let the hot water run over her body as she cried. Grieving for her loved one she'd lost to gun violence in Chicago, her tears mixed with water, ran down the drain. While KI was crying and sobbing, she didn't hear Big Carl enter the bathroom and step into the shower with her, until he wrapped his arms around her waist, causing her to jump.

"What's wrong, baby girl? You cool?" Big Carl asked, seeing she had been crying.

"I have to go. My friend was killed last night."

"Damn, baby. Straight up? Is it anything I can do?" Big Carl asked, trying to be supportive.

"Yeah, just drop me off, Carl. I got to go," KI said, stepping out of the shower. Her sadness was quickly turning into anger. Big Carl obliged KI's wants and after they were both dressed, they checked out of the Crown Plaza and headed back to Chicago. The two-and-a-half-hour ride back to the city was a quiet one. KI was lost in her own thoughts as Big Carl drove down the Dan Ryan Expressway. KI told him to get off at her mom's house on 59th and Bishop, but when Carl didn't get off on the exit he was supposed to, she looked at him with a perplexed look.

"Why didn't you get off on 51st?" Big Carl looked over at him with a sinister look stretched across his face.

"You ever heard of a nigga named Roy, shorty?" he asked. At first, the name did not register right away, then it was as if her thoughts were in slow motion. The Homicide Crew had robbed and killed Roy over his money and drugs. Looking at Big Carl, she now knew where she had seen him before. He was with Roy that night when Roy picked her up. *"That's my man's Killa. I gotta drop him off at his car up north. Then we can do us."* KI played the conversation back in her head. Big Carl was Killa. KI cursed herself for not being strapped. She really never left home without her pole. She was slipping and now her slipping had her naked in a time of danger.

"Stupid bitch, thought niggas wasn't gone find you niggas. That work y'all took from my man, I hope it was worth y'all lives," Big Carl growled before he pulled a gun out of his jacket and slapped KI across the head viciously with it, causing it to split instantly. KI passed out from the blow.
Her head laid against the tinted passenger side window, leaking profusely.

KI was awakened from her slight coma when somebody opened up the passenger door. Big Carl grabbed a handful of KI's dreadlocks and forcefully snatched her out the vehicle. It was 4:00 in the morning and they were in an alley on the city's west side. Big Carl had been riding around, trying to find somewhere to off KI, until he pulled into the dark alley off Sacramento Street. KI tried to weakly fight Big Carl off, but he was just simply too strong. He dragged her behind a dumpster and forced her at gunpoint to her knees.

Raising his gun to the back of her head, KI did something she never thought she would do, said a silent prayer to God. Big Carl pulled the trigger, blowing KI's brains out. She felt nothing before she was sent to complete darkness. Big Carl tucked the hot .40 back on his waist, before hopping back in his whip and fleeing the murder scene.

KI had set up Big Carl's homie, Roy, to get robbed and killed. The game god had blessed his game when he bumped into KI at the mall. The way the streets spoke on KI's name made her sound like a diabolical mass murderer. To Big Carl, she was nothing more than a freak bitch who tried to play in a man's game, and found out the hard way, everything ain't for everybody. Unfortunately, this lack of knowledge had cost her, her life.

CHAPTER 26

TWO YEARS LATER

"Yaton Anderson, report to R&D immediately. I repeat, Yaton Anderson, 07505-424 report to R&D immediately," the officer said over the loudspeaker in the unit. Today was the day YaYo had been waiting for, for eight and a half years. Today, YaYo would be released back to society. He had come through the Federal Bureau of Prisons immature and wild.

Now, he knew how to stop and think and strategize all situations. He was going home with more of a boss mind frame. YaYo and Nino had both completed the S.M.U. program and got transferred to different penitentiaries. Nino was transferred to USP Hazelton in Virginia and YaYo was shipped to USP Beaumont in Beaumont, Texas.

YaYo and Nino had built a solid relationship by being in the small cell together for over eighteen months, a lot of them. Nino was his brother and he was going to hold things down in the end. Even though Nino had a life sentence, YaYo would never turn his back on him. He forever had a friend.

YaYo had also been keeping in touch with Mr. B through their way mail. YaYo would send mail to his mom and she would mail it to Mr. B and Mr. B would do the same. YaYo was also in contact with Ms. Sanchez and his son, Jamari. He already accepted Jamari as his own, but he still wanted a blood test to make sure Ms. Sanchez had no problem with it.

As for Shakira, to YaYo's surprise, she did not condemn him after he confessed to getting a correctional officer pregnant. But it did hurt her heart to know that she and Shamira would have to share YaYo with another. But Shakira was understanding. YaYo had a life sentence when he did what he did. He was only human and who was she to judge? They worked through it and Shakira couldn't wait until her man came home so they could be a family.

YaYo heard his name over the loudspeaker and made his way to the officer station. He was having a flashback when he was released from juvenile prison after serving time on a body. YaYo was stopped by a few other good men to give him dap and show love. He had only been at USP Beaumont for about a year, so he didn't mess with a lot of dudes. YaYo wasn't the friendly type. Prison and life situations had taught him that friendships had to be built through trials and tribulations, but at the same time he was cordial and respectful to those who showed the same characteristics.

After showing love to the real niggas on the unit, YaYo was escorted to the administration building. Once in the building, YaYo was taken to the captain's office. The captain held YaYo's face card in his hand.

"State your name and registration number," the captain said with authority

"Yaton Anderson, 07505-424," YaYo responded. The captain looked over the face card again before he shook his head approvingly.

"Alright, Mr. Anderson. Good luck and stay out there, the world is beautiful." The captain stuck his hand out to YaYo to shake his hand. YaYo looked at his hand for a second, then shook hands with the captain, showing humility. The captain had read YaYo's file. He knew the inmate was a gangster. Aggressive, but yet righteous and he carried himself like a man, so the captain respected him for that.

YaYo was then escorted to a holding cell where he would have to wait for the U.S. Marshals to come get him to take him out to the airport in Beaumont, where he would catch a flight back home to Chicago. The feds gave YaYo seven hours to get to the halfway house on the west side of Chicago. The halfway house was mandatory for anybody being released from federal custody.

YaYo had no property. All he had was a brown folder containing his paperwork. He had on a brand-new gray jogging suit and on his feet a fresh pair of dark gray New Balance. YaYo had grown his beard and had it lined to perfection, his bald head was crispy clear as the Palmer's Cocoa Butter lotion faced its slight shine.

He was ready to be released to the streets. He had a mission to accomplish. YaYo had made Mr. B a promise he vowed to keep by all means. If it wasn't for Mr. B, YaYo would have died behind the walls of the penitentiary. He was done with the life of crime. He needed to be there for his family and be the role model they needed him to be, it was all about trying to live positive, a prosocial lifestyle.

YaYo sat in the holding cell, vowing to never return to prison. He just hoped the cold Chicago streets that made him wouldn't force his hand to go back to how he used to be.

Quavon was on a plane headed back to Chicago, coming from California. He went down there to check on one of his dispensaries. He had one in Orange County, California, Los Angeles and one in Beverly Hills. The business was going smooth and the numbers were up and that was all he cared about.

He had been on federal supervision for only eighteen months of his three-year sentence. After obtaining steady employment and not having any dirty piss tests, Quavon's P.O. let him off supervision after only serving half. The G.B.C. was keeping the numbers up in the streets. Choppa had been strictly standing on the business, so niggas knew not to play with that money. Playing with that Nation work would get you fucked up.

After hard work and dedication, The Get It Boy Clique was able to pay Castilino for the bricks they owed for and in return, Castilino flooded them with more bricks. Castilino gave Quavon some good solid advice. "Quavon, always stop and think before you make a decision that will reflect the outcome of your life, learn from your errors, and communication is most important when conducting business." With a consistent plug, the G.B.C. was getting to a bag. The Homicide Crew had tried their hand and found the Get It Boy Clique's gangsta was not to be tested.

Quavon sat on the plane glued to his Instagram. He couldn't believe what he had just heard. YaYo had just been released from prison. Quavon was geeked. *Why didn't bro let me know he was coming home today?* Quavon thought. Whatever the reason he was glad he was home. He couldn't wait to show his brother what he had accomplished, now he could take his seat at the head of the table and eat. Little did Quavon know, his brother was on a whole other path.

__To Be Continued...__
YaYo 4
Coming Soon!

Submission Guideline

Submit the first three chapters of your completed manuscript to ldpsubmissions@gmail.com, subject line: Your book's title. The manuscript must be in a .doc file and sent as an attachment. Document should be in Times New Roman, double spaced and in size 12 font. Also, provide your synopsis and full contact information. If sending multiple submissions, they must each be in a separate email.

Have a story but no way to send it electronically? You can still submit to LDP/Ca$h Presents. Send in the first three chapters, written or typed, of your completed manuscript to:

LDP: Submissions Dept
Po Box 944
Stockbridge, Ga 30281

DO NOT send original manuscript. Must be a duplicate.

Provide your synopsis and a cover letter containing your full contact information.

Thanks for considering LDP and Ca$h Presents.

Coming Soon from Lock Down Publications/Ca$h Presents

BOW DOWN TO MY GANGSTA

By **Ca$h**

TORN BETWEEN TWO

By **Coffee**

THE STREETS STAINED MY SOUL **II**

By **Marcellus Allen**

BLOOD OF A BOSS **VI**

SHADOWS OF THE GAME II

By **Askari**

LOYAL TO THE GAME **IV**

By **T.J. & Jelissa**

A DOPEBOY'S PRAYER **II**

By **Eddie "Wolf" Lee**

IF LOVING YOU IS WRONG… **III**

By **Jelissa**

TRUE SAVAGE **VII**

MIDNIGHT CARTEL III

DOPE BOY MAGIC IV

By **Chris Green**

BLAST FOR ME **III**

A SAVAGE DOPEBOY III

CUTTHROAT MAFIA II

By **Ghost**

A HUSTLER'S DECEIT III

KILL ZONE **II**

BAE BELONGS TO ME III

A DOPE BOY'S QUEEN II

By **Aryanna**

YAYO 3

CHAINED TO THE STREETS III
By **J-Blunt**
COKE KINGS V
KING OF THE TRAP II
By **T.J. Edwards**
GORILLAZ IN THE BAY V
TEARS OF A GANGSTA II
De'Kari
THE STREETS ARE CALLING II
Duquie Wilson
KINGPIN KILLAZ IV
STREET KINGS III
PAID IN BLOOD III
CARTEL KILLAZ IV
DOPE GODS II
Hood Rich
SINS OF A HUSTLA II
ASAD
TRIGGADALE III
Elijah R. Freeman
KINGZ OF THE GAME V
Playa Ray
SLAUGHTER GANG IV
RUTHLESS HEART IV
By Willie Slaughter
THE HEART OF A SAVAGE III
By Jibril Williams
FUK SHYT II
By Blakk Diamond
THE REALEST KILLAS

S. Allen

LIFE OF A SAVAGE IV
By **Romell Tukes**
QUIET MONEY II
By **Trai'Quan**
THE STREETS MADE ME II
By **Larry D. Wright**
THE ULTIMATE SACRIFICE VI
IF YOU CROSSM ME ONCE II
By **Anthony Fields**
THE LIFE OF A HOOD STAR
By Ca$h & Rashia Wilson

Available Now

RESTRAINING ORDER **I & II**
By **CA$H & Coffee**
LOVE KNOWS NO BOUNDARIES **I II & III**
By **Coffee**
RAISED AS A GOON I, II, III & IV
BRED BY THE SLUMS I, II, III
BLAST FOR ME I & II
ROTTEN TO THE CORE I II III
A BRONX TALE I, II, III
DUFFEL BAG CARTEL I II III IV
HEARTLESS GOON I II III IV
A SAVAGE DOPEBOY I II
HEARTLESS GOON I II III
DRUG LORDS I II III

CUTTHROAT MAFIA
By **Ghost**
LAY IT DOWN **I & II**
LAST OF A DYING BREED
BLOOD STAINS OF A SHOTTA I & II III
By **Jamaica**
LOYAL TO THE GAME I II III
LIFE OF SIN I, II III
By **TJ & Jelissa**
BLOODY COMMAS I & II
SKI MASK CARTEL I II & III
KING OF NEW YORK I II,III IV V
RISE TO POWER I II III
COKE KINGS I II III IV
BORN HEARTLESS I II III IV
KING OF THE TRAP
By **T.J. Edwards**
IF LOVING HIM IS WRONG…I & II
LOVE ME EVEN WHEN IT HURTS I II III
By **Jelissa**
WHEN THE STREETS CLAP BACK I & II III
THE HEART OF A SAVAGE I II
By **Jibril Williams**
A DISTINGUISHED THUG STOLE MY HEART I II & III
LOVE SHOULDN'T HURT I II III IV
RENEGADE BOYS I II III IV
PAID IN KARMA I II III
By **Meesha**
A GANGSTER'S CODE I &, II III
A GANGSTER'S SYN I II III

YAYO 3

THE SAVAGE LIFE I II III
CHAINED TO THE STREETS I II
By J-Blunt
PUSH IT TO THE LIMIT
By **Bre' Hayes**
BLOOD OF A BOSS **I, II, III, IV, V**
SHADOWS OF THE GAME
By **Askari**
THE STREETS BLEED MURDER **I, II & III**
THE HEART OF A GANGSTA I II& III
By **Jerry Jackson**
CUM FOR ME I II III IV V
An **LDP Erotica Collaboration**
BRIDE OF A HUSTLA **I II & II**
THE FETTI GIRLS **I, II& III**
CORRUPTED BY A GANGSTA I, II III, IV
BLINDED BY HIS LOVE
THE PRICE YOU PAY FOR LOVE
DOPE GIRL MAGIC I II
By **Destiny Skai**
WHEN A GOOD GIRL GOES BAD
By **Adrienne**
THE COST OF LOYALTY I II III
By Kweli
A GANGSTER'S REVENGE **I II III & IV**
THE BOSS MAN'S DAUGHTERS I II III IV V
A SAVAGE LOVE **I & II**
BAE BELONGS TO ME I II
A HUSTLER'S DECEIT I, II, III
WHAT BAD BITCHES DO I, II, III

SOUL OF A MONSTER I II III
KILL ZONE
A DOPE BOY'S QUEEN
By **Aryanna**
A KINGPIN'S AMBITON
A KINGPIN'S AMBITION **II**
I MURDER FOR THE DOUGH
By **Ambitious**
TRUE SAVAGE I II III IV V VI
DOPE BOY MAGIC I, II, III
MIDNIGHT CARTEL I II
By **Chris Green**
A DOPEBOY'S PRAYER
By **Eddie "Wolf" Lee**
THE KING CARTEL **I, II & III**
By **Frank Gresham**
THESE NIGGAS AIN'T LOYAL **I, II & III**
By **Nikki Tee**
GANGSTA SHYT **I II &III**
By **CATO**
THE ULTIMATE BETRAYAL
By **Phoenix**
BOSS'N UP **I , II & III**
By **Royal Nicole**
I LOVE YOU TO DEATH
By Destiny J
I RIDE FOR MY HITTA
I STILL RIDE FOR MY HITTA
By **Misty Holt**
LOVE & CHASIN' PAPER

YAYO 3

By **Qay Crockett**
TO DIE IN VAIN
SINS OF A HUSTLA
By **ASAD**
BROOKLYN HUSTLAZ
By **Boogsy Morina**
BROOKLYN ON LOCK I & II
By **Sonovia**
GANGSTA CITY
By **Teddy Duke**
A DRUG KING AND HIS DIAMOND I & II III
A DOPEMAN'S RICHES
HER MAN, MINE'S TOO I, II
CASH MONEY HO'S
By Nicole Goosby
TRAPHOUSE KING **I II & III**
KINGPIN KILLAZ I II III
STREET KINGS I II
PAID IN BLOOD **I II**
CARTEL KILLAZ I II III
DOPE GODS
By **Hood Rich**
LIPSTICK KILLAH **I, II, III**
CRIME OF PASSION I II & III
By **Mimi**
STEADY MOBBN' **I, II, III**
THE STREETS STAINED MY SOUL
By **Marcellus Allen**
WHO SHOT YA **I, II, III**
SON OF A DOPE FIEND

Renta
GORILLAZ IN THE BAY **I II III IV**
TEARS OF A GANGSTA
DE'KARI
TRIGGADALE I II
Elijah R. Freeman
GOD BLESS THE TRAPPERS I, II, III
THESE SCANDALOUS STREETS I, II, III
FEAR MY GANGSTA I, II, III
THESE STREETS DON'T LOVE NOBODY I, II
BURY ME A G I, II, III, IV, V
A GANGSTA'S EMPIRE I, II, III, IV
THE DOPEMAN'S BODYGAURD I II
Tranay Adams
THE STREETS ARE CALLING
Duquie Wilson
MARRIED TO A BOSS… I II III
By Destiny Skai & Chris Green
KINGZ OF THE GAME I II III IV
Playa Ray
SLAUGHTER GANG I II III
RUTHLESS HEART I II III
By Willie Slaughter
FUK SHYT
By Blakk Diamond
DON'T F#CK WITH MY HEART I II
By Linnea
ADDICTED TO THE DRAMA I II III
By Jamila
YAYO I II III

YAYO 3

A SHOOTER'S AMBITION I II
By S. Allen
TRAP GOD
By Troublesome
FOREVER GANGSTA
GLOCKS ON SATIN SHEETS
By Adrian Dulan
TOE TAGZ I II III
By Ah'Million
KINGPIN DREAMS I II
By Paper Boi Rari
CONFESSIONS OF A GANGSTA
By Nicholas Lock
I'M NOTHING WITHOUT HIS LOVE
By Monet Dragun
CAUGHT UP IN THE LIFE I II
By Robert Baptiste
NEW TO THE GAME I II
By **Malik D. Rice**
LIFE OF A SAVAGE I II III
By **Romell Tukcs**
LOYALTY AIN'T PROMISED
By Keith Williams
Quiet Money
By **Trai'Quan**
THE STREETS MADE ME
By **Larry D. Wright**
THE ULTIMATE SACRIFICE I, II, III, IV, V
KHADIFI
IF YOU CROSS ME ONCE

By **Anthony Fields**
THE LIFE OF A HOOD STAR
By **Ca$h & Rashia Wilson**

BOOKS BY LDP'S CEO, CA$H

TRUST IN NO MAN

TRUST IN NO MAN 2

TRUST IN NO MAN 3

BONDED BY BLOOD

SHORTY GOT A THUG

THUGS CRY

THUGS CRY 2

THUGS CRY 3

TRUST NO BITCH

TRUST NO BITCH 2

TRUST NO BITCH 3

TIL MY CASKET DROPS

RESTRAINING ORDER

RESTRAINING ORDER 2

IN LOVE WITH A CONVICT

LIFE OF A HOOD STAR

Coming Soon

BONDED BY BLOOD 2

BOW DOWN TO MY GANGSTA

S. Allen